A Royal Proposition

THE ROYAL HOUSE OF ATHARIA

TAMARA Gill

COPYRIGHT

A Royal Proposition
The Royal House of Atharia, Book 2
Copyright © 2021 by Tamara Gill
Cover Art by Wicked Smart Designs
& Chris Cocozza Illustration
Editor Grace Bradley Editing
All rights reserved.

ISBN: 978-0-6452047-8-0

*P*rincess Alessa of Atharia was not so certain now that she had entered the London Season that her choice to come here was one of her best plans. With her eldest sister busy ruling Atharia as the new queen and her adoring husband never far from her side, Alessa's royal duties would be better served elsewhere. Thankfully her sister had agreed.

Truthfully, Alessa had wanted adventure. To leave Atharia for a time and see some of the world herself. London had been her choice, but the Season was not at all what she expected.

She was staying in London with Duke Sotherton and his sister-in-law, a widow, Lady Bagshaw, acting as her chaperone. It had started swimmingly. A lovely London townhouse, happily situated on Piccadilly in Mayfair, she was where everyone who was anyone wished to be.

What Alessa had not expected were her two guards, who shadowed her every move while at her entertainments. If the burly men had their way, they would follow her into the retiring room, she was sure.

She sighed, watched as the many men, all eligible gentlemen for a woman in her position, walked past without an offer to dance, to converse, or anything at all. And she knew the reason why. They stood at her back, arms crossed, glaring at everyone who passed.

Lady Bagshaw, Aunt Rosemary as she liked to be called, cast a curious glance over her shoulder. Her ladyship more than aware of Alessa's annoyance at her sister's demand that she have two guards to keep her safe during the Season. Why she could not just use Marco, whom she'd known since she was a young woman, was beyond her. No, her sister hired a new guard, an Englishman who knew his way about London and was willing to use blunt force to keep her safe.

She stemmed the shiver that threatened to tremble down her spine at the thought of the English brute who stood to her left. Never had she seen a scarier man, muscular and tall, his shoulders strong enough to lift her with one hand, she was sure, and without breaking into a sweat.

How was it that there were such men in England? She had always thought the men to be a little pasty white, a genteel type of man. The one behind her would certainly choose whisky over a cup of tea.

"Why you must have these guards in the ballroom is beyond me," Aunt Rosemary said, casting another quick look over her shoulder at the men at their backs. "They really will impede your chances of marriage, I think. Why, the men here this evening are already scared of them."

Alessa sipped her wine, only too aware the guards at her back were as annoying as a pebble in her silk slipper. "My sister insisted upon it. There are reports of men here in England who still sympathize with my uncle's cause back in Atharia, and I, therefore, must be guarded. An absurd notion, for I have not felt the least bit threatened."

Aunt Rosemary frowned. "But did he not pass away? I thought the attempt to overthrow your sister was finished with, now that he is no longer about."

They had hoped it was over, but yet again, even from the grave, her uncle had reached out a selfish, decaying hand to attempt a coup. In Alessa's opinion, a waste of time as her home country, Atharia, was prospering under her sister and her new husband's rule. The country was alive again. People were free to increase their wealth through work and travel, and not have a corrupt monarchy breathing down their necks, telling them what they could and could not do, how to spend their money or raise their children.

Who would not want such a free life? To follow her uncle's evil regime made no sense at all—an unforgivable act.

"He did pass away, but I suppose there are those who are unable to let go the fact their evil plot did not come to fruition and seek revenge. I do not think they will try anything silly against me, but my guards are here to stay, and there is little I can do to dissuade my sister from requiring them."

Aunt Rosemary leaned close, dropping her voice to a whisper. "The English one, he is very handsome for a guard. Maybe I should put myself in peril if it means such a specimen will follow me about town."

Alessa choked on her sip of wine, coughing to cover her laugh. "You are too wicked, but as for your statement, I have no opinion. He was vetted and hired by our royal aids. When I arrived at Sotherton Estate, he was waiting for me along with Duke Sotherton. We traveled to London

the following day, and the guard has not left my side since."
And becoming quite the inconvenience if she were to
consider any of the gentlemen here in England for
marriage. She was used to Marco lurking in the background, but the Englishman, Mr. Oakley if she remem-
bered correctly, seemed different. More obsessed over
being about her person.

"I thought to speak to the duke about them guarding
your door at night. Surely they would sit at the stairs at the
very least. To me, guarding your door almost gives your
location away to any intruder."

Alessa frowned, unaware they remained so close to her
person at that time, but she supposed one of them always
stood guard, as was their employment. "You are right in
your observations. I would welcome you speaking to the
duke about the arrangement." The thought of the English
brute standing at the ready, not a few feet from her when
she was gowned in nothing but a shift made heat kiss her
cheeks. Would his dark, hooded, gaze warm at the sight of
her dressed in such a way?

Alessa downed her wine, wondering where that
thought had come from. A man of no wealth or power was
not whom she or her family would ever allow her to marry.
No matter how devastatingly handsome or how alluring his
dangerous demeanor made him to the opposite sex.

She was royal and expected to marry well. Alessa
caught sight of Wyatt, Earl Douglas, coming toward her.
She felt the approach of her protectors closer to her back
as his lordship bowed before her and Lady Bagshaw. She
smiled, giving him her hand in welcome. Wyatt was a sweet
gentleman, and there was a time when she thought she felt
more for him than one would feel for a friend, but she had
long ago decided otherwise.

They were friends, yes, and she hoped they would remain so. He had been so very helpful to her during her uncle's coup attempt last year. But there was little attraction between them. She had seen how much her elder sister adored her husband, her eyes warming every time they were together.

She wanted that as well.

She wanted to burn for her husband. Never did she wish to marry, simply because the gentleman was appropriate or titled or wealthy. Such a union would never work.

"Your Highness, Lady Bagshaw, how very fortunate we all are that you're here this evening. Will you do me the honor of dancing with me, Princess Alessa?" Lord Douglas asked, a genuine smile on his lips.

Alessa inclined her head, allowing him to lead her out onto the floor. "Thank you, yes. That would be very nice." The music commenced, a waltz her favorite dance. She threw herself into the dance, enjoying the music and the man who was also her friend.

She supposed that was one of the main reasons she no longer saw Lord Douglas in a romantic sense. He reminded her of a sibling more than a potential lover and husband.

"You look very beautiful this evening, Princess Alessa. I hope you do not take offense to me saying so."

"Not at all," she replied. How could anyone dislike being told they appear beautiful? The last year in Atharia had been hard, no balls and parties, no meeting the people of her homeland. She had been a prisoner and treated far beneath her station and what she ought to be afforded as a princess. The degradation, the insults, and the slurs were never-ending when her uncle ruled. To be here now in London, in a sweet gentleman's arms who wanted to dote on her and dole out compliments was just the thing. "You may flatter me to your heart's content, my lord."

He grinned, a look that ought to make a woman's heart flutter. Her heart did not, nor would it ever for this man. She would have to tell him soon that there was no future for them. He would be disappointed, of course, but it was for the best. He ought to move on, court another more willing lady and gain the great love she knew he wanted.

"Have I told you that I'm so very happy that you're in London this year? I know you have not had an easy time, but as a peer of the realm, I do hope we're making your stay here in England enjoyable."

Alessa glanced about the room at the other dancers surrounding them, not wanting to appear more attached to the man in her arms than she was. Until she found that special one who made her blood pound fast in her veins, she would have to guard her reactions and words.

Lord Douglas pulled her into a turn, and her gaze settled on her English guard. Rowan was his name, and it suited him, she decided. He watched her dance. His mouth pulled into a disapproving line, a severe frown between his brows to the point it looked as if he were about to strike someone—or wanted to.

He was so very severe all the time, and yet something about him captured her attention.

"I am enjoying myself very much," she replied jovially.

"Your guards are not an impediment? They watch you like hawks."

Alessa couldn't agree more, but there was little she could do about it now. Having guards was a given, since she was a princess. It was just a shame they could not be more inconspicuous. "That is the employment my sister hired them to do, so I suppose it would be odd if they did not."

"Of course," he agreed, "but to be honest with you, Princess Alessa, no gentleman wants those two brutes breathing down his neck."

She giggled. All points she was well aware of. Mayhap she ought to start making Marco and Mr. Oakley stand outside the ballroom doors instead of at her back. Was his lordship trying to tell her in the nicest way possible that the reason he was continually asking her to dance and no one else was because they were fearful over her guards, and he was not? He had dealt with similar situations last year in Atharia.

Something had to change, and it would not be her.

The waltz came to an end, and she dipped into a curtsy, welcoming when Lord Douglas led her back to where Lady Bagshaw stood.

Lord Douglas did not remain and excused himself when Mr. Oakley glared at his lordship with so much loathing it was almost palpable.

Alessa had enough. She walked up to her guards, close enough that only they would hear her words. "This must end. I cannot have you both standing behind my person, night after night, scaring off the gentlemen who may wish to court me. I shall never meet anyone if you two are always glaring and growling at everyone."

Marco threw her a pitying glance, but Mr. Oakley merely crossed his arms over his chest, puffing himself up and making himself look larger still. How was he able to look taller and more muscular all of a sudden?

And why did the sight of his large upper arms make her mouth water?

Absurd behavior.

7

"We do apologize, Your Highness, but we are under orders. Unless you are safe and stowed in your rooms at Sotherton's London townhouse, you must be within our presence and view at all times. That is our queen's decree, one we cannot break," Marco said, pity in his tone.

Alessa crossed her arms, mimicking the English god staring down at her as if she were some annoying gnat he wanted to squash.

"Would you prefer that you are killed, Princess?"

She did not miss the Englishman's condescension, and nor was it missed by Marco.

"Watch your tone when speaking to Her Highness," Marco said, his voice like steel.

Mr. Oakley's lips twitched as if amused by being reprimanded by Marco. "I am working for your sister the queen under direction by the government here in England. I do not take nicely to playing babysitter to a royal who wishes to flout about England and accomplish little other than finding a husband. I shall keep you safe, but I will not flatter you or declare utter devotion at your feet simply because you are a princess. If you dislike the way I work, feel free to replace me at your earliest convenience."

Alessa felt her mouth gape, and she shut it, her teeth chattering at the impact. Marco bowed to her. "If you would excuse us, Your Highness. We shall be within view. We merely need to discuss the particulars of moving you on to your next ball."

"Of course," she said, still unable to believe her English guard had dared talk to her in such a way. No one spoke to her in that manner.

If she were not so very shocked, she might have been a little proud of the man.

CHAPTER 2

*R*owan Oakley, a lad from the streets—where a sly look or stolen loaf of bread could mean you lived your last day on earth—never bowed down to toffs. He'd grown up rough, dirty, and hungry a lot of the time until he'd been old enough to look after himself. To gain alliances, bribe those who did not want to cooperate, or kill those who dared to cross him.

He glowered at the little princess, who thought her perfect Season was in jeopardy due to their presence. The fool had no idea who he was or why he was at her side, night after night, day after day. She would not think herself so high and mighty if she knew just how close to danger she really was.

How was he to ensure he remained in her employment? That was the question he ought to be asking himself.

He glared harder at the princess and was happy when she paled a little at his inspection of her.

Coin. The coin was the reason he'd taken on this soul-numbing job. The offer of so much blunt, more than he'd ever seen in his life, was too good to walk away from. Even with the risks involved.

And there were many.

This employment would give him a new start, far away in the Americas, where no one knew or cared who he was. England was full of risks, threats of the past coming back to haunt him. He needed to get away, let his mind forget things that no man or child wanted to remember.

He read the room, unable to imagine living the life of a toff. All the rules they needed to abide by. Not that all the gentlemen behaved as they should. Some he had recognized from the filthiest brothels in London. He doubted the ladies dancing within their arms would appreciate knowing where their cocks had been.

Lord Douglas one of the worst offenders to haunt the gambling hells and brothels in London. Rowan couldn't help but wonder how the fellow's dick hadn't already fallen off since he was so enamored with a whore named Fanny, a woman known to carry the pox.

Princess Alessa, however, was a beautiful woman, tall and luscious, ripe for the picking. She was probably as stiff and chaste as the women in the room, if truth be known. Lifeless in bed as well as conversation.

He could not think of anything duller than night after night of such entertainments. How any of them could stand the banality of this life was beyond him.

"There were reports that Roberto Delenzo has been seen in London as he was the closest confidant to Her Highness' late uncle. I think it's safe to say he is not here for any other reason but to strike at Princess Alessa," Marco said to him, his gaze fixed on the princess as it always was.

Rowan already knew Roberto Delenzo was in town and the reasons behind his traveling to England. Rowan was at this ball, following a princess' skirts about London due to Roberto's orders and blunt. Money that would secure his future once he carried out the plan.

He caught sight of the princess laughing, her eyes alight with hope and happiness. It was all a show and as fake as those who danced around her. None of these people cared for others. They took. They never gave. What was one less princess to have to pander to in this world? Nothing. No one would miss her. Hell, no one would miss any of these high handed bastards.

His whole life, he had been at the mercy of the rich. As a young boy, the protections that age brought with it were not there. He'd suffered, and he would not suffer again. If it meant that one rich, spoiled daughter or son was eliminated to gain his freedom, to never live in fear and poverty, then he would do it.

"It is suspicious, I would agree," Rowan stated, his tone bored. "The princess is well-guarded. They will not get to her unless through us." *Or by us*, he inwardly snickered. The fools. All of them. Stupid to think the princess was so safe.

Little did they know, they had let the lion into the cage, and he would devour them all if he had to, to get what was promised him.

The waltz came to an end, and Lord Douglas escorted Princess Alessa back over to them. Her displeasure at their presence gave him an amused sense of gratification. That the men who wished to court her did not do so because of her guards at her back was as enjoyable as the money promised him for ridding the world of another useless, spoiled being would be.

He listened to their polite, ridiculous conversation

regarding nothing of importance before his lordship took his leave.

Rowan studied her from behind. She was a tall woman, her hair sun-kissed and coiled up atop her head in larger curls, a pretty diamond tiara worth a king's fortune glistened in the candlelight.

So much wealth and privilege. How they lived with themselves when so many others suffered, he would never understand. Without warning, she turned and stormed up to them, chastising them both over their presence.

Rowan crossed his arms over his chest, not the least amused by her outburst. "We do apologize, Your Highness, but we are under orders. Unless you are safe and stowed in your rooms at Sotherton's London townhouse, you must be within our presence and view at all times. That is our queen's decree, one we cannot break," Marco said, always trying to please and appease the spoiled little brat.

He would like to bend her over his knee and spank her ass. The idea was not helpful, and he frowned.

Alessa crossed her arms, mimicking him. How he'd like to crush her and her self-importance like a gnat. "Would you prefer that you are killed, Princess?" His tone oozed with disdain.

"Watch your tone when speaking to Her Highness," Marco said, his voice hard.

Rowan fought to keep a smile from his lips. "I am working for your sister the queen under direction by the government here in England. I do not take nicely to playing babysitter to a royal who wishes to flout about England and accomplish little other than finding a husband. I shall keep you safe, but I will not flatter you or declare utter devotion at your feet simply because you are a princess. If you dislike the way I work, feel free to replace me at your earliest convenience."

Her mouth gaped and he grappled with the image of that mouth against his. She had the sweetest pink lips. What a shame they belonged to a woman such as herself.

Marco bowed to her. "If you would excuse us, Your Highness. We shall be within view. We merely need to discuss the particulars of moving you on to your next ball."

"Of course," she said, watching him keenly.

Rowan followed Marco, and they stood beside a bank of windows, still within view of the princess but far enough away to ensure privacy. "You cannot speak to Her Highness in that way or tone. She deserves respect. She is a good person, and you are employed to do a job, and that is all. Keep your mouth shut, or the Crown will be forced to replace you and reprimand you if you do not toe the line."

He nodded, playing the part of a chastised man, bowing his head. "I forget how to speak sometimes around these types. I will apologize to Her Highness," he lied, having no intention of doing such a thing.

Marco watched him a moment, and Rowan could see he was debating whether to believe him or not. "Very well," he said, his stance relaxing somewhat. "See that you do." He paused. "It's time I did a check around the grounds. Try to not argue any further with the princess, or anyone else for that matter."

Rowan saluted him and went to stand behind the princess once again. Lips closed, ready to play his part until an opportunity arose to do what he was being paid for.

She turned, pinning him to the spot. "I can feel you are looking at me, guard," she spat, having never used his name, even though they were introduced when he first started working for her family. "Is there something wrong with my gown, or is there something you wish to say to me that you keep on looking at my person?"

He chuckled, unable to stop himself from laughing at her meaningless words. "I was merely checking to ensure you had not caught anything from his lordship Douglas."

She gasped, turning on her heel to face him. Rowan ground his teeth. The princess ought to be taught a lesson. Who did she think she was standing up against him, trying to shove him back in his place? Intimidate the poor like the high-handed toff she was. He had no place in this world, no loyalties, nothing, which made him more dangerous to her than anyone.

Silly little rich royal.

"What do you mean by that, guard? I will not have you disrespect my friends in such a manner by talking about them when you do not have the right."

He raised one brow, staring down his nose at her. The princess had a bite, after all. Granted, it was similar to a bite of a small puppy, but at least she wasn't entirely pathetic. "I shall speak in any way I choose, Princess. I'm here to do a job, keep you safe, and that is all," he lied. "I was not hired to simper and flatter those who wish to simper and flatter you."

Her mouth gaped again, and he tore his gaze from her full lips. They had the smallest amount of rouge upon them, just enough to darken the natural shade, but it was enough to make her utterly beautiful to look upon. Not that he needed to think of her as anything but a job to be done. A woman to remain close to. To have the trust of her people before doing the job he was hired to do.

Kill her.

She stepped closer still, and he fought not to lean into

14

her, let her feel the strength of himself. Let him feel her sweet breasts up against his chest. They rose and fell with each annoyed breath she took, and his lips twitched. It was enjoyable irritating the little termagant.

"Well, guard, should you wish to keep your position at my side, I suggest you shut your mouth and only speak when spoken to. Is that understood?"

He glared. Never did he allow toffs to speak to him in that way. Hell, he did not allow anyone to speak to him so offensively, but he needed to tonight. He would get his revenge on her eventually when he snuffed out her life, but he needed to stay where he was until then. "Whatever you say, Princess," he quipped, turning his attention to the guests and ignoring her.

She turned on her heel, taking a glass of wine from a passing footman and downing a good portion of the drink before her tense shoulders seemed to ease.

He rolled his own, having never taken well to others pushing his buttons, and the princess aggravated him by merely looking in his direction. The sooner he removed her from this world, the better.

His life awaited him, and he wasn't sure how much longer he could stand living in this fake, glittering world. Not long if the last of his nerves were saying anything about the fact.

*L*ater that evening, Alessa sat in her bedroom in her shift and nightdress, staring out at the man who wandered about the gardens, cheroot in his mouth and gun hidden somewhere on his person as it always was.

How she wished she was better equipped to handle the

English giant ass who was assigned to her side for the duration of the Season.

If ever there was a man whom she loathed, it was this one. "Beast," she spat aloud, knowing he was too far away to hear, but it made her feel better all the same to mumble the slur.

She shook her head. Whyever would he take the position in the first place if he loathed her so much? Which was in itself an odd thing because everyone loved her. Or at least they seemed to when they were talking to her. She had heard nothing but high praise since she arrived, so why this man, a guard of all people, thought bad of her she could not fathom.

"Beast," she mumbled again, catching sight of herself pouting in the window.

She huffed out a breath. She would have to do something to change his opinion of her. What to do was much harder to think upon when she did not know why he hated her in the first place. She was kind and with a happy disposition. What wasn't there to like?

Her secretary, an older gentleman who had once worked as a junior aid to her late mama, walked into her room, bowing. "Your Highness, the trip to the women's shelter proposal site has been scheduled for next week. Are you in agreement?"

She turned away from the infuriating man in the garden and faced Mr. Todd. "Of course, yes. That will be fine."

Mr. Todd marked off something in his notebook at her words. "Have we found who owns the orphanage we're looking to acquire yet?" she queried, knowing that owner was a lot harder to locate than a pin a haystack.

"Not yet, Your Highness, but we are still inquiring."

"Good," she said. "Was there anything else that requires my attention before I retire?"

He shook his head. "No, that was all I needed to discuss. Goodnight," he said, departing the room, closing the door quietly behind him.

Alessa walked back to the window, the prickly Mr. Oakley no longer in the gardens. She pursed her lips. What to do about him, on the other hand, was still yet to be determined.

CHAPTER 3

The Season was invigorating and more enjoyable than Alessa had thought it would be. Of course, she was used to parties and balls, but being new to London, wanting to meet as many people as she could after being cossetted for so long in Atharia was a thrill unlike any she had ever known.

She had decided to ignore her two guards who growled and watched everyone as if there were a multitude of assassins waiting to strike at her.

Thankfully her time in London had been uneventful to date, even with the warnings to her sister the queen before she left Atharia that her deceased uncle had allies in England who may wish to do her harm.

Such threats had not come to pass, and nor would she worry about them unless they did. London was her time to enjoy herself and possibly find a suitable husband. She would not let the past dictate her future.

Alessa had watched from afar as others danced numerous jigs, minuets, and cotillions, but she longed for a waltz to be included like every other eligible debutante.

The Duke Hamilton stood across the ballroom from her, his gaze one of interest, that even she could read well enough. He was not the most handsome man in the room, but he may well be one of the most influential.

He started toward her, and butterflies took flight in her belly. Would he ask her to dance? Perhaps the waltz was to be next. So many men did not ask because of who she was and her two guards standing behind her. How wonderful if this man had more initiative than others.

The duke bowed before her just as the orchestra started playing the first notes to a waltz. "Would you like to dance, Your Highness?"

Alessa slipped her hand into his, nodding her acquiesce. "I would like that very much, Your Grace." He led her out onto the floor, sweeping her into the dance before another word was spoken. She laughed, having not expected him to be as playful as he was influential.

Other couples soon joined them. Alessa met the duke's eye, studying him. "You dance very well, Your Grace. How lucky the young ladies in London are this Season to have such a dance partner who excels at sweeping them about the ballroom floor with such ease."

He chuckled, and she had to admit that His Grace was a lot more handsome when he smiled than when he did not. Perhaps she could look at him as a potential partner in life. Certainly, with his being a duke her family would not refuse, and he seemed pleasant enough.

She glanced over his shoulder and caught sight of her English guard watching her. His dark, hooded eyes were too hard to read. She could not make that fellow out at all, not that she needed to. He was her guard, but still, being near her so often, the man who was hired to keep her alive, she would like to know him a little. Believe that he was honest and responsible.

Something told Alessa he did not want to be known, not by her or anyone.

"I do try to please on the dancefloor, Princess Alessa," His Grace answered, pulling her from her thoughts. "But you must be pleased to be in London. I hope you will stay the entire Season. We should so hate to have you leave us before we were able to know you properly."

She beamed up at him. How lovely he was to say such a thing, and she loved nothing more than making new friends and acquaintances. "I will be here for the entire Season unless I'm called home, which I do not think will be the case. Everyone has been so welcoming and kind. I do like it here very much."

"Mayhap you will make England your home instead of Atharia." He grinned down at her. "As a matter of fact, I have been to your homeland. A beautiful country and one to rival my own, I'm certain, but not quite as good."

Even better. The man was more surprising than she thought. "Well, it is certainly warmer than England, but I cannot agree with you. Atharia is the best place to live. I'm very fortunate."

"No," he said, pulling her closer to his person as he guided them about a turn at the top of the ballroom floor. "It is I and the society we circulate in who is fortunate to have you all to ourselves this year."

Alessa smiled but did not reply, unsure she ought to encourage him too much. She did not know him at all, or anyone for that matter. She was yet to find a gentleman who sparked an ounce of interest in her, other than mild, friendly amusement, the duke no different.

She had hoped coming to England that she too would

find a handsome, lovely gentleman like her sister Holly and marry him. So long as he was titled and from a similar background to her upbringing, she was certain her family would have no issues with her chosen one.

The dance came to an end, and the duke returned her to her guards, both Marco and the Englishman standing with legs spread and arms crossed.

Alessa rolled her eyes, standing between them and feeling like the most absurd person here for their trouble.

The duke took his leave, and she rounded on them. "Marco, please check the grounds and house. I'm certain I'll be more than safe here with one guard during a ball instead of two."

"Of course, Your Highness." He bowed and left.

She turned to the Englishman. His dangerous gaze made her shiver, and she wasn't entirely sure she could trust this man. There was something about him that made her question him.

Or perhaps you ought to question yourself because he intrigues you like no other.

Alessa shoved the unhelpful thought aside, narrowing her eyes on his that continued to watch her like a hawk.

"Like I said the other evening, you do not need to remain so close to me. I'm perfectly safe here at the ball. No one will attack me here, Mr. Oakley."

His lips thinned into a displeased line, and she noticed for the first time they were fuller than she expected, a lovely shape, in fact, perfect for kissing one would think, if one were inclined to kiss such a man.

She was not one of them. She'd never kissed anyone, and nor would she until the day of her wedding. Or at least until she found someone she wanted to kiss before taking such vows.

"As I declared, Your Highness, I will not be leaving you alone. My position in your household is to keep you safe. To ensure that remains so, I must be here with you at all times."

She turned, facing the throng of guests, noting yet again that other than the duke, no gentleman ventured her way. Her guards really were becoming the most restrictive chaperones. "Lady Rosemary is just over there, keeping a close eye on my person, Mr. Oakley. I'm certain you could wait over near the ballroom doors or some other such place."

He shifted behind her, she could not see, but she sensed that he'd moved to clasp his hands behind his back. A movement both the Englishman and Marco often did when wanting to stand their ground. That his shifting sent a thrill down her spine and shivers across her skin, she refused to acknowledge.

Alessa took a deep breath.

"I'm certain that will not be happening, Princess."

Alessa waited for her name to drop after the honorific, but it did not come. She turned to face him, stepping closer than she ought. "It is not just princess though, is it, Mr. Oakley?" she reminded him.

A flicker of amusement entered his dark-gray gaze. "Alessa," he finished, and she wasn't certain which was worse—that he had only used her title, or when her given name fell from his lips.

Her body warmed at the sound of her name from his person. Whatever was the matter with her? Why was she reacting to the man and not the eligible gentlemen such as the duke she just danced with?

It made no sense at all. "You play with fire, Mr. Oakley.

I would suggest you stop your nonsense with my name and remember your place."

His brows rose, his face hardening at her words. "Of course, Princess Alessa. Whatever you say."

She turned on her heel, starting for the refreshment table. The man was infuriating, but worse, she did not like the fact he had made her mad, and then she'd sounded all high and mighty. Even if she were born to wealth and privilege, she had never grown up believing she was above anyone else in the world. She would have to apologize.

Why she had said such things in the first place, she could not fathom. Never had she played the royal card against anyone in her life. Alessa picked up a glass of Capillaire and took a sip of the orange-flavored drink, setting it back down almost immediately as the thick, syrupy drink was too sweet for her.

She felt Mr. Oakley's presence at her back and turned, facing the crowd. "I apologize, Mr. Oakley. I do not think myself above you in any way. I did not mean to offend."

He did not reply, but she could feel him judging her. Without saying a word, she knew he did not believe or accept her apology. "I'm here to keep you safe, Princess Alessa. I do not care for the opinion of you or anyone who is here. Do not think that I am wounded by your words, for I am not."

She felt her mouth gape. No one had ever been so honest with her in her life. Or rude. In a matter of a few days, this man seemed to think it was perfectly acceptable.

"I was only trying to make amends between us. I do not want to be enemies with you, but you certainly make it very hard not to be so."

He scoffed, watching the crowd. Alessa felt like

stomping her foot like a child that he would not look at her.

"We are not enemies. We are nothing at all."

She left him and walked from the room, needing air. She spotted a door left ajar and strode straight for it, making the darkened servants' passage just as her guard caught up to her. He clasped her arm, stopping her from going too far along the darkened gallery.

"You need to return to the ball," he demanded, his voice dark and as dangerous as she had ever heard it.

"I need a moment away from you. I apologize for being rude yet again, but you were utterly obnoxious when I was trying to be nice. I think you ought to leave me be for a time."

He stepped closer to her than he ought. Annoyance and obstinance ran through her like water, and she refused to step aside and let him think he had power over her. She was the princess here. She had the power to determine her own life, not him. Alessa moved her attention from his shirt and loosely tied cravat over his cutting jaw and displeased line of his lips to meet his eyes. "The door back to the ballroom is that way," she pointed, making her demand known.

*R*owan could do it now. In his mind, he played over the scene of removing her from the earth forever. Of taking her innocent life, and all for the blunt he was promised. Enough to remove him from poverty, to never have to starve or fight for survival. To be safe from those who wished to harm him, and those who had already harmed him in his life.

He stared down at Princess Alessa. Her captivating

24

features arrested him more than they ought. He reached out, cringing as his hands touched her soft cheeks, slipping about her neck. She would think he was going to kiss her, but he was not.

One flick of his wrists, and she'd be dead and without a sound to alert those close by.

Her chest rose and fell with labored breaths from her flight from the ballroom or from his touch, he did not know. He did not want to know either, he told himself, and yet, instead of snapping her small neck as he should, he found himself slipping his fingers into her hair, drawing her closer. "I'm not going anywhere, Princess," he heard himself say, his tone soft and cajoling.

What was he doing? He was hired to kill the woman in his arms, not seduce her.

Defiant as usual, stronger than he'd ever thought her to be, she raised her chin, pinning him with a cold glare. "Are you not? What do you think you're about to do, Mr. Oakley, with my person? Kiss me, seduce me? Make me forget that you're an ass and that I'm annoyed at you?" she taunted him.

He growled at her words, the wrong ones to say right at that moment. He wrenched her closer. Her breasts bounced into his chest, her gasp a whisper against his lips. "You think I could not seduce you to my will, Your Highness?"

He heard her swallow, her eyes wide with alarm, but still the defiant minx he was beginning to appreciate bit back at him. "You're no gentleman. Why would I think you would start acting like one now?"

His lips quirked. "Why indeed."

CHAPTER 4

*W*hat was she doing? He was no gentleman at all. She could not kiss her guard, a man no more than a servant in her home. She could not kiss him here in the dark, secluded passageway at a London ball. Not anywhere. The man was a menace, a rude, bossy ass whom she did not like.

And yet, she did not move or step out of his reach as his head dipped toward hers. Her stomach clenched, delicious warmth pooled between her thighs, and Alessa found herself clasping the lapels of his coat, holding him close instead of pushing him away.

Had she gone mad!

Utterly insane if she were honest with herself. No, her mind screamed, but her body had other ideas about removing herself from this predicament. It purred and leaned against him, enjoyed the roughness of his coat against her silk gown. Her nipples beaded, her breasts ached for his touch.

And she wanted him to kiss her. She wanted to feel the touch of a man like she had longed to for so long now.

He dipped his head farther, his lips brushing hers with a softness that made her toes curl in her silk slippers. She had expected him to be hard and rough, demanding and coarse, as he was in the flesh, and yet, his kiss was nothing of the sort.

His lips settled over hers, coaxing her to kiss him back. She needed no urging. She had dreamed about kisses for so long that even if her first was with her guard, she would not run from it, but toward it with open arms.

Alessa opened for him, giving him what he urged from her, and the axis of her world tilted. She gasped at the intimacy of their embrace, the smooth, silky glide of his tongue against hers. His hand as it tightened about her hair, the soft growl that hummed from deep in his chest.

She felt all at sea but glorified in every moment of the kiss. His arm enfolded her, holding her close. She smelled the citrus scent of his cologne, the hardened muscles of his chest, the frantic beat of his heart.

Alessa reached up, standing on tiptoe, and wrapped her arms about his neck, following his lead with the kiss and giving him what he wanted. Her surrender.

The embrace was wonderful, liberating, and she craved more. So much more. She wanted to kiss and be kissed in just this manner until she took her last breath.

How wonderful it was, all new and exciting.

His mouth melted on hers, deep and hard, leaving her breathless. Alessa found herself moving before her back came up against a wall. He strained against her, his chest teasing hers, and she gasped, having not expected her body to burn for his touch, his commands to do as he bade her.

Her nerves sizzled, her breath hitched, her body ached.

Alessa moved against him, seeking him in a way she had never sought anyone before in her life. How could she react in such a way and all from a kiss? But what a kiss it was.

His hand skimmed her waist, her back, to clasp the globe of her bottom. She moaned when he kneaded her flesh there, drawing her against him. Alessa knew enough about the male form that she understood what she felt straining against her stomach.

Had she made him so?

He ground against her abdomen, his manhood tempting her in a way she had not thought possible only a half hour before.

The sound of laughter broke through her haze of seduction, and Mr. Oakley wrenched away, stumbling almost in his haste to remove himself from her.

He gazed down at her, dazed, his eyes wide with shock. Alessa did not say a word, unsure what either of them could say right at this moment. They had simply kissed if a kiss could be termed with such platitude, but she knew it could not be.

Best to say nothing at all, she decided, watching and taking her cues from him. She had never been in such a situation before. Surely Mr. Oakley had been and would know what to say and do.

Would he kiss her again? Or was he debating tugging her back to the ball and depositing her there, away from him and out of his reach?

"Return to the ball, Your Highness," he said, his tone cold and lacking the emotion that his kiss had sparked within her soul.

Alessa tipped up her nose and strode away, determined not to let him know or ever see that his easy dismissal of her and what they had just shared hurt her heart.

The kiss she experienced with her guard was the first-ever in her life. He could at least have pretended to like her a little after the fact.

But he was an ass, after all.

*R*owan fisted his hands at his sides and did not watch as Alessa strode away from him as if she cared not a hoot for the kiss they just shared. Not that he gave her much inclination to feel anything but loathing for him, but still, he would have thought she would have had some kind of reaction to his touch.

For by God, he had felt as though his world had changed the moment his lips touched hers. If he had his way, he would have taken more liberties, kissed her into submission, and wherever that led them. Had the ball not impinged on their interlude, she would still be in his arms and at his mercy.

He stared down the dark passage, unsure how it was that he had kissed her instead of taking the opportunity afforded him to do what he was being paid to do.

Kill her.

Alone, here in this part of the house that seemed unused this evening, it would have been easy to snap her sweet, innocent neck, but he could not bring himself to do it. She had looked up at him with such need, such innocence, that all thoughts of hurting her fled his mind.

A deep, menacing chuckle sounded somewhere along the darkened hallway before a dot of red light appeared. A man lit a cheroot, coming into view before leaning against the wall with an unhurried air.

"Well, well, well, how very surprising to see you so well-acquainted with Princess Alessa. I did not think seducing the woman was a requirement for the job that you have been hired to complete."

Rowan faced down Fred, one of the many underhanded criminals who worked for Roberto Delenzo, who hired him. If the fellow thought to intimidate Rowan, he was mistaken, being several inches shorter than himself. "Isn't a chap not allowed to sample the goods before they're discarded? Nothing wrong with me seducing the wanton princess if she is willing. It will enable me to gain closer access to her than I have had previously. I may even be able to get her alone a time or two, out of Marco's ever-vigilant gaze."

The man's beady eyes narrowed as he thought over his words. Rowan hoped he bought his ploy, for the last thing he needed was Fred or anyone else disbelieving his words and seeing him as another who needed to be eliminated from this world.

How are you going to kill her now that you've tasted her sweetness?

That, Rowan did not know, and now was not the time to debate his moral code. If only there were another way out of the poverty nightmare he'd lived in all his life. He had done a lot already to remove himself from it, too many killings, thievery, and brute force upon targets, but there was always more he could do to secure his future. Legal jobs that did not involve any of those harsh treatments.

But to kill a woman for blunt?

That kind of job was new, even for him. Rowan inwardly cringed, not so sure he could finish the job he was hired to do. To date, no one had ever cared for him in his past. Not when he was a child or now as a man. He was nothing to all these toffs, royals, and even the underhanded criminals such as the one standing before him.

But to kill the princess when she had done nothing to deserve such an end? When it was not her fault he'd been born into such a shitty life?

"Is that all this is? A bit of fun under her skirts before we're rid of her?"

Rowan started back toward the ballroom, wanting to remove himself from the conversation, and before he gave himself away that it wasn't just a dose of fun.

"I loathe the woman and her kind. I will do what you have asked me. Do not spy on me again, or you may find yourself at the end of my gun barrel."

The man chuckled, sucking once again on the cheroot before throwing it in Rowan's direction. "Be sure to complete the job you're to be paid for. Have your fun if that is what you want, but do not cross us, or you'll find yourself at the end of *my* barrel when you least expect it."

The man slinked into the darkness. Not a sound came from his footsteps, and a shiver of unease slithered down his spine. He knew when he'd accepted the job that he was walking into a lion's den—playing into the hand of the ruthless cutthroats like himself. But the blunt promised had been too large a sum to give up.

The image of Princess Alessa floated through his mind, and he ran a hand over his jaw. He had not expected the woman to be so beautiful, and there was something about her warmth when talking to others that he had not seen when around the *ton* before.

A niggle of doubt settled in his mind that she was different. That had he known she was not the daughter of a tyrannical regime in Atharia he would not have taken the order. He'd been lied to, he was sure of it.

31

He strode back into the ballroom and spied Marco, watching their charge, who danced about the ballroom floor, her smile warming a dark, cold place in his chest that had never felt anything.

What was it about this woman that he savored? Why did he care? Why had he kissed her?

He came and stood beside Marco, watching her like so many others in the room did.

"The passageway clear?" Marco asked him, his accent thicker than that of Alessa's.

"Yes, nothing but servants going about their chores." They watched as Alessa moved on to her next dance partner. "There is a rumor the Queen of Atharia is not the correct heir for the homeland. What do you know of the family and what happened last year?" Rowan asked, needing to know.

Marco did not look at him, nor did he miss the grimace that twitched over his features. Marco told him of Princess Holly's flee back to her homeland after being ambushed in England. Of her hiding at Duke Sotherton's estate and her growing bond with the Marquess Balhannah, now king consort. Of how Princess Alessa was forced to flee her royal home after the mistreatment of her uncle. Her fear for her sister, who had been left behind.

The uncle sounded like a crazed man who did not know how the line of succession worked in Atharia. Women could inherit and rule there. The man had no basis for his claim. And the men here in England who still carried the torch of revenge for their downfall, their failed coup, had no basis to kill Alessa.

He had signed a deal with the devil, and now that devil wanted to be paid.

The princess caught his eye, and like a punch to his

gut, he felt the full force of her inspection of him over her dance partner's shoulder. He looked away, not wanting to admit he had made a mistake. That no amount of money was worth the death of a woman wholly innocent.

However was he going to step away from this predicament?

CHAPTER 5

*A*lessa was in serious trouble. Since the past week after her devastating kiss with her English guard, she had not been able to stop thinking of him. Of his lips against hers, his touch as he held her gently in his arms before the seduction of the embrace made them lose their heads.

Certainly, she must have lost her mind even allowing such liberties. What would her sisters think?

Alessa clasped her stomach as it fluttered at the thought of the kiss. Her cheeks still stinging with emotion. And yet, Mr. Oakley, Rowan as she thought of him now, had continued on with his employment as her guard, cold and aloof as ever, keeping watch of her at balls and parties and not attempting to kiss her again. It was enough to drive her insane.

Did he not think about this kiss as she did? Did he not want to do it again?

She nibbled on her fingernail, staring out the windows of the downstairs morning room. Her guards were about, Marco stood just outside the door to give her a little privacy while she took some time for herself in solitude, but all her attention was on the man who strolled past the windows every few minutes.

Her sisters would tell her to stop being absurd. That there was no chance she could look at such a man for a husband. Her sister had married a lord, a future duke. She would not be allowed to marry a man with no title or money to his name.

Her life did not work that way, no matter how much she may wish it did.

Aunt Rosemary bustled into the room, a footman only a few steps behind carrying a tray of biscuits and a fresh pot of tea.

"Your Highness, good morning. I thought we would go over the invitations that have arrived this morning and take tea together."

Alessa was pleased with the distraction. She needed all the distraction she could get if she were to get over her infatuation with her guard.

"That would be lovely," she said, smiling. "And please, do call me Alessa when we're alone. The honorifics are not needed here. I know well enough who I am."

Her ladyship chuckled, pouring two cups of tea and tipping a small droplet of milk in hers just as she liked it. "Old habits die hard, Alessa, but I shall try to remember to do as you asked."

"Thank you." She sipped her tea, sighing at the refreshing blend before leaning back in her chair, her gaze slipping to the windows as Rowan walked past once again.

"You have several invitations that I think you ought to consider—one of them a night opera at Covent Gardens, which I think will be entertaining. I had a similar event when I had my coming out, many years ago now," the older woman said with a chuckle. "My mother, God rest her soul, would tell you it was the night she lost me in the park and thought I was lost forever to scandal."

"And were you?" Alessa asked, leaning forward, having never heard Aunt Rosemary say much about her life, since she was a spinster.

"No, thankfully, I had merely run into a friend, and we started talking, and my party had moved on. When they did not see me with them, they panicked."

Alessa chuckled. "Forgive me for asking, but you never remarried after your husband passed away, which, if I'm not mistaken, was quite young. Did no gentleman ever catch your eye a second time, or was marriage not an occupation you enjoyed?"

Aunt Rosemary stared off into space, her mind clearly lost in the past. "I was asked again, but he was nothing like my first husband, and I grew nervous about the whole thing. He was not of the *ton* and certainly not rich enough. My sister married a duke, you see, and I knew my family, no matter how many marriages I had, expected a certain social standing."

Alessa could understand wholeheartedly what Aunt Rosemary was saying. "I feel that way too sometimes. My sister married a future duke, even if the family would have preferred a prince," she said, catching Aunt Rosemary's eye. "Not that we do not love Drew, for we do, but he was not whom a queen ought to consider as king consort. Not from a social standing point of view in any case."

"How lucky Holly and Drew are that their union is a love match," Aunt Rosemary stated, a wistful smile on her face.

Alessa knew better than anyone just how much her sister adored her husband. They were the perfect match, and she wanted the same. "I had hoped that by Holly marrying a duke, I would have a little freedom of choice as well, but I'm surrounded by dukes and earls, vain viscounts, and boring barons. None of them spark an ounce of interest. I fear I shall return to Atharia and be married off and sent to live on the continent with a foreign prince."

Lady Rosemary frowned as she bit into a biscuit. "I presumed you were favorable to Lord Douglas. Has something happened that you no longer welcome his suit?"

The memory of her kiss with Rowan floated through her mind, and she felt heat warm her cheeks. "We have become friends, but other than that, I do not feel any deeper emotions for his lordship. I think he understands and feels the same." She paused, playing with the muslin on her dress. "There is someone who has caught my attention, but he would not be suitable for the family."

"The family, my dear, do not have to marry the man you choose. You do. You have to live with your choice. You must make the correct one, or you'll suffer the consequences your entire life, and that is no life at all."

Alessa thought over Aunt Rosemary's words. She would be the one who would have to live with and love the man she married. To commit to the wrong gentleman would be disastrous. She wanted to be as happy as her sister Holly was with Drew. She wanted to share secret glances and touches when they thought they were alone and no one was watching.

She wanted love.

Rowan strolled past the window yet again, and her heart beat fast. The man, as infuriating, obstinate, and argumentative as he was, had been so very different when wrapped in her arms. She had certainly felt something for him, but did he feel anything for her in return?

Or was she merely a number in a long line of women who no doubt threw themselves at him?

Was she being a fool wanting him as she did? She bit aggressively into a biscuit. Rowan may not feel anything at all for her. He may be utterly unaware that she was indoors, thinking of him, remembering his kisses, and wanting more. He may have already kissed another since kissing her. He had been absent from the home yesterday, and she had been rattled, wanting to know where he had gone, who he was with, and not being able to ask.

"Thank you for your insight, Aunt Rosemary. I shall consider your words further and try as hard as I can to make the right choice."

The terrace door opened, and in strolled the man himself. He bowed but did not meet her eye, and disappointment stabbed at her. She ground her teeth, hating that he could be so cold and aloof while her body sizzled at the mere sight of him.

Aunt Rosemary had asked her if she had found anyone who interested her, and she had. But he was not a man she could ever consider. No princess married a man of little means and connections, a guard, hired to keep her safe.

*R*owan swapped locations with Marco and took to guarding the princess indoors. The past week had been hell. To be around the chit when all he wanted to do was lock her away in a room and have his way with her delicious self had maddened him beyond what he could endure.

He had requested a day off yesterday and was granted the leave, intending to slake his amorous desires with a willing doxy. He had instead returned to his lodgings on

The Strand and had stared at the walls and ceiling for twenty-four hours.

He could hear the princess talking to Lady Bagshaw, an amusing woman if ever he knew one. A widow who was well-liked by society and her family, the princess no exception as they seemed to get along very well. Their laughter made his lips twitch.

He schooled his features. What was wrong with him that he smiled at the inane chatter of women? He was here to do a job, one that he knew he could not complete. But how to pretend to keep her at a distance, be immune to her charms? He needed to think out how to keep her safe from those who did wish her to die. To stop their plans against a woman who did not deserve such punishment.

He was a traitor, both to the princess and the man who had hired him. The only way forward was to remove the threat, thug by thug, and then leave England forever. He could not stay here after turning against such powerful peers.

Lady Bagshaw strolled past him, the scent of verbena wafting across his senses. He fought not to turn and glance into the room to see what the princess was doing.

Was she sitting alone, watching him? Was she bowed over parchment and quill, writing to her family as he so often caught her doing? Her golden locks hanging down against her back when she was home and in private. He couldn't help but wonder what she was like when she was in Atharia, a regal and powerful princess.

Did she allow her hair to fall free there too, or did she tie it up in pins and diamonds as he'd often seen at balls and parties? So much wealth, so much power, and opulence. One of her diamond clips could set him up for life, and yet, she stuck it in her hair without a by your leave, without care if she lost or misplaced it.

He could not fathom such a world, such a life.

Soft footsteps sounded on the Aubusson rug that lay within the morning room before she strolled past him. Without thought, he grabbed her hand, wrenching her back into the room and shutting the door before anyone caught them.

His lips were upon hers in an instant. She stilled in his arms before she melted against him, her mouth as insistent as his, opening for him like a flower. He kissed her hard and long, thrusting his tongue against hers. Wanting to make her his, not just now, but forever.

He wasn't sure where that thought came from, and he ignored it the moment she made a sweet little sound of need that went straight to his groin. He hoisted her against his hips, placing his aching cock against her mons. She squirmed, rubbing against him, and he ground back, eliciting another moan from her sweet lips.

"I want to fuck you," he admitted, his mind a whir of thoughts, his body uncontrollable with need.

She lay her head against the wall, her breath coming in quick succession. "We cannot."

Her words doused him like a cold bucket of ice water, and he set her down, stepping back and righting his rioting emotions. Of course, she did not feel the same way. She was royal. He was a nobody. That he had even asked her was an absurd notion he had no right even to imagine.

Rowan opened the door, and without another word, she bolted from the room. Her hurried footsteps away from him loud in his ears.

What the hell was he doing? He could not say such

things to a princess. With her cossetted upbringing, he doubted she even knew what his words had meant.

He stepped out into the foyer, needing to follow her upstairs to guard her door. To think and plan.

Five thugs in total worked for the mastermind loyal to Alessa's deceased uncle. He would remove each of them before taking out the one who hired him. Then and only then would he leave London and the princess to the life she was born to live.

He would travel to the Americas. Start a new life there, possibly marry and have a family, away from the poverty, the dangers of England, and the temptations of a princess who could never be his.

CHAPTER 6

A week later, Rowan had the first opportunity to deal with the men who sought to injure the princess and take her life.

He cursed the day he had agreed to be one of them. He had always killed for survival or because those who met their end at the end of his blade deserved what they had coming to them. As a child who grew up on the streets, unprotected by family or blunt, he knew only too well the horrors that were dealt out to boys and girls without a voice. Without protection.

He had been one of them, and that fear deep inside him that had settled there years ago had jumped at the opportunity to gain the wealth needed to remove him from that cesspit forever.

The princess's only crime had been that she was born into a rich and powerful family—a royal family and daughter to a king. At first, he had been curt, cruel even, and talked down to her station and decree, but it had only been to protect himself, to keep her at arm's length. If he did not know her, he would not care what happened to her.

He could no longer think like that. She had wiggled under his skin, and he could not remove her, no matter how hard he tried.

Rowan caught sight of Mattia. The oldest thug hired to assassinate Alessa, should he fail to do so. The chap liked to slink around the docks and often stole onto ships in the dead of night and removed precious stock that was yet to be delivered. He also had a liking for violence against women, while enjoying the company of his own sex.

Rowan leaned against a crate, shadowed by the buildings and cloudy night sky, and watched as Mattia was buggered by an unknown man who had crossed his path.

He would be easy to pick off in the throes of pleasure, but Rowan wasn't a monster, and nor did he want the other man to see what he was about to do. He would allow them to finish before he slit Mattia's throat.

Hearing the sound of them parting ways, he slipped the long, sharp blade from his pocket, careful to keep it hidden as he stepped out before Mattia, halting his steps.

"Evening, Mattia, having a pleasant time, I see," he said, pulling into step with his intended victim.

"Piss off, Oakley. Got nothing to do with ye what I do with me time," he said, not looking at Rowan.

"A little birdie told me that you'd been down at The Raven Tavern, beating up on the barmaids there. Care to explain why?" he stated, his tone light but with an edge of steel.

Mattia halted and turned to face him. "You mean Lucy? She been pissing in yer ear, has she? Did she mention that the meal she served me last week was nothing more than muck scraped off the top of the Thames? She deserved what she got."

"Really?" Rowan stated. "She said you held her down

on a table and seared her face with the fire poker. A bit extreme for an unsatisfactory meal."

Mattia chuckled, a menacing sound if ever he heard one. "Wench deserved it. Not worth anything anyway. None of them are." Mattia rubbed a hand over his jaw. "What are you doing down here anyway? You're supposed to be killing that bitch princess. If you don't, I will, and I'll enjoy putting a hot fire poker on her face too before I run her through."

A wave of anger, uncontrollable in its ferocity, ran through Rowan, and he grabbed Mattia by his throat, throwing him up against a nearby warehouse wall. "You'll not touch one hair on the princess's head. Do you understand?" he declared, towering over him.

Mattia chuckled. "I'll touch more than her hair, boy."

Out the corner of Rowan's eye, he saw Mattia reach for his pocket, but he was quicker. With no hesitation, he swiped his blade across Mattia's neck, not even flinching when the blood splattered across his face. Mattia grabbed for his throat, trying to stem the flow of blood, but it was little use. The cut was deadly, and he would die. It was just a matter of time.

He gurgled as he choked in his last few moments on earth. Rowan watched, caring little for the sight but wanting to ensure he died before he left. "Doesn't look like you will touch anything on the princess now," Rowan stated, as Mattia's eyes dimmed as his life left his body.

Rowan strode away, throwing the blade into the Thames and ridding himself of the situation and one of the thugs hired to hurt Alessa. One down, five to go.

. . .

*T*he opera at Covent Garden was an evening that Alessa could only have dreamed about when she was locked up in Atharia under her uncle's illegal rule. Lanterns hung from the trees surrounding the stage, the music as enchanting and beautiful as the gardens. The scent of roses, lavender, rosemary, jasmine, and wisteria were a delight to the senses.

They had arrived and set themselves up in a private pavilion. The duke and Aunt Rosemary seated at her side as they listened to the entertainment. People were everywhere, a lot of the *ton* had their own pavilions as they did, but the general populace, wanting an evening of culture, stood before the stage, danced, and enjoyed the entertainment.

Her two guards stood behind her, and she was highly aware of one in particular. There were others, of course, out within the crowd, keeping watch and willing to protect her at the cost of their lives, but there was only one who kept her mind reeling, her heart beating like a mad drum.

Aunt Rosemary complimented the soprano to Alessa, and she nodded in agreement, but the talented woman could not keep her attention on stage. The light touch of Rowan otherwise engaged her mind. The feel of his finger sliding against the top of her arm enough to make her lose her mind.

Alessa closed her eyes, wanting him with a need that scared her. After their kiss last week in the morning room, she had rallied herself to behave. To not long for his touch, his mouth against hers, taking her to a place that was forbidden and not real life. To give other gentlemen the chance to win her heart.

The week had been utterly tedious and without success.

She was doomed, and the man at her back was the reason behind her failure.

She adjusted her seat, effectively ridding her of his touch, and she felt him move away, ceasing his teasing. She missed his touch immediately, and Alessa cursed herself a fool.

Whatever was she going to do?

A scream rent the air, and in an instant, she was in Rowan's arms, settled at the back of the pavilion and out of sight of those present this evening.

She took a calming breath, waiting to hear what the commotion was about, but then she recognized just where she was and with whom.

He cradled her against his chest, his face, his lips too close for comfort. This was so wrong. He wasn't for her, could never be hers, but oh, please Lord save her, she wanted him.

The sound of Marco's voice demanding an answer from those who patrolled the grounds floated to her, but she no longer cared what was happening out the front of the pavilion. All she cared about was that they were alone, unable to be viewed by anyone. Never had she ever wanted to kiss a man so much in her life.

Alessa cupped his jaw and brought her lips to his. He met her halfway, taking her mouth and kissing her with such ferocity that it left her breathless. Oh yes, this is what she had wanted all along, what she had longed for this past week. How had she stayed away from him, kept him at arm's length?

She could no longer do so.

His hand slid up her back to cup her neck. His fingers massaged her there, sending shivers up her spine as the kiss turned savage. Her breasts ached, her body wept between her thighs for his touch. It was too much and not enough. This would never do. She would expire before returning to Atharia if she did not have more of this man.

"Meet me near the dark walk. I must be alone with you."

Alessa shook her head, knowing that would be impossible. "You know I cannot. How will I leave here without Aunt Rosemary accompanying me?"

He frowned back toward where her chaperone sat behind a curtain. "Ask for me to escort you on a stroll."

Marco's voice declared that all was well, that it was merely a woman being overzealous with her lover. Alessa wished she could have such freedom as the nameless lady. Even so, she found herself nodding in agreement with Rowan instead of telling him no.

Rowan set her down, and she poked her head about the curtain, meeting Marco's gaze. "Is it safe for me to return to my chair?" she asked her guard.

The large, concerned gazes of the duke and Aunt Rosemary met her eyes, and her heart went out to them. She supposed they were not used to such dangers on their charges, but life for a princess was never an easy one, no matter what others thought on the subject. And hers was worse than most with her uncle's henchmen rumored to be still determined to do the family harm, even here in England.

"All is safe, Your Highness. Please return to your seat," Marco said.

She spied Rowan come about the pavilion and meet Marco out front. They spoke for a time before returning to stand behind her as they were before.

The opera came to an end, and an orchestra started to play, and dancing commenced. For a time, they watched all levels of society eat, drink, and dance, rendezvous and enjoy themselves as they too drank wine.

"I would like to go for a stroll if you agree, Lady Bagshaw. May one of my guards escort me? I should so like to look about the gardens a little."

"I should come with you," she declared, but Alessa waved her concerns aside. "No one will be watching, not here. There are so many others here, dancing and making merry. I shall remain in the light. Nothing will happen to me, I promise. A little normalcy, if you would be so gracious to allow it."

Aunt Rosemary seemed to object, but then nodded her acquiesce. "Of course, Your Highness, but just this once."

"Thank you," she said, standing. "Mr. Oakley, please escort me for a walk. I wish to see what Covent Gardens has to offer. Marco, please remain here."

Rowan bowed, helping her down the two steps off the pavilion before escorting her away. Alessa ignored the odd look Marco gave her at her request. She would have to be careful not to look too forward or seem inclined between Rowan or Marco in the future. She did not need her guard becoming suspicious of her.

They walked about the dancers for a time, stood, and listened to the orchestra as it played a waltz. How she wished she could dance with Rowan. Be swept about the outdoor ballroom floor in his arms.

"Can you dance?" she asked him, curious.

He looked out at the throng of dancers and nodded. "I can, but not as well as the gentlemen out there. I was self-taught, not the best tutor, I'm sure you would agree."

She hated that he had struggled in his life. There was something about him that she knew was dark and danger-ous, a part of him that had fought for survival, but how and why he had to work so hard, she did not know. Did he have any family? Was he an only child? Where were his parents? She knew so little about the man that fascinated her so.

"Will you dance with me?" she asked him, wanting to be in his arms, not beside him or in front of him, but with him, safe in his hold.

"I cannot dance with you here, Your Highness."

His use of her title reminded her that she was not some genteel lady without a role in this world, and she could not waltz so publicly with her guard. As much as that fact irritated her to no end, it did not mean they had to dance here.

"There is a copse of bushes behind us. We could dance there, and no one would ever know."

Rowan glanced over his shoulder and spied the foliage she spoke of. He held out his arm, and she wound hers through his as he escorted her farther into the gardens.

The shadows of the grounds enfolded them as they stepped out of sight and a shiver of expectation stole across her skin. He pulled her against him with a slow, seductive air that left her breathless.

She could not understand why, when around this man, she was not herself. That she no longer wanted to conform to social rules or her family's expectations. She wanted him and no one else.

A madness that would not abate, and nor did she wish it to.

CHAPTER 7

They were but yards from the revelry of Covent Gardens, and yet, here in the shadows of the garden, no one knew they were there, out of sight and away from prying eyes.

Just as Rowan preferred his life to be.

Alessa was all softness in his arms, her alluring silk gown made his blood pump fast, and as for her lips, they were made for kissing. She stared up at him in the moonlit night, all but begging without words for him to close the space between them and kiss her.

He pulled her close, the scent of jasmine teasing his senses. Rowan lowered his head, giving her time to change her mind, to leave, but she did not. Instead, she wrapped her arms around his neck and met him halfway.

Her mouth opened on a sigh, and he took the opportunity to deepen the embrace. She was delicious, wanton, and made the sweetest little mewling sounds as their tongues teased, tasted, and relished their dance. He had never responded to a woman as he responded to Alessa.

A princess. So far above him and out of his league. That she was even kissing him, a street urchin, hardened by time and the mistreatment of people who ought to know better, he could not understand.

He had been hired to get close to her, infiltrate her security and kill her. He could not kill her now. Not because she was everything lovely and right in his arms, but because she was a good person. Wealthy, yes, spoiled perhaps and indulged for certain, but she was also kind, honest, and did not judge.

A rare gem, to be sure.

Her uncle's henchmen were fools to think that killing Princess Alessa would solve all their troubles. It would only make them double. He would not allow them to injure one hair on her pretty head.

She pulled back, running her palm along his jaw. "Your kisses have ruined me for others, I fear."

Ruined her? He would never look at another woman the way he looked at Alessa. If he ruined her for all time, he was right there alongside her. "I'm not for you, Princess," he said, needing to remind them both that what they were doing, the kissing and petting, was not sustainable. At some point, she would return to Atharia, marry a prince. He would be in America, thousands of miles from her, never to see her again.

The thought made his stomach lurch.

"Why are you not?" she asked him—no mocking in her tone. "You are a man and one whom I like quite a lot if you had not already noticed. Why can we not be together?"

He sighed, pulling her against him and holding her close. "Because I'm your guard, a nobody, and you are a princess. A woman of royal blood who has expectations and priorities that are greater than this. Or what we make each other feel."

She studied him a moment, and he wondered what she saw. Did she see a man who wished what he had said was not true? That a princess could marry a once-homeless street boy without a penny to his name. That she could love a man who was once hired to kill her. How could she like anything about such a man? He loathed himself for being the traitor he was.

"I do not want to be with anyone else, and so I would ask that until the pressures of my life, or my time here in England comes to an end, that we steal these precious times together and enjoy them as much as we can. Could you do that small favor for me at least?"

He kissed the top of her head, the scent of wild berries teasing his senses. He'd never known a woman to smell so nice. "If we're caught, you'll have a scandal unlike any you've ever known. I'm not worth such a risk, Alessa. I truly am not."

She leaned up, touching her lips to his. "You are worth the risk to me."

Her words unlocked a part of him that he had kept hidden away, would not allow seeing the light of day until now. He seized her mouth, kissing her until his mind whirled uncontrollably.

She met his kiss with equal fervor, and he never wanted to stop. Never wanted to watch as she sailed away out of his life. She clung to him, and he fought for control, to rein in his needs and take what he wanted. She was a princess, a lady, a maid. He had to remember those facts.

But when she pushed herself against him, all but purring against his hardened cock, all restraint fled.

. . .

*A*lessa ached between her thighs. Her body did not feel like itself. It wanted to climb up on Rowan and do wickedly delicious things with him. Things she did not know but most definitely could feel.

Her body was alight with need, and she knew he knew how to please her. But would he? Would he give her what she wanted, knowing who and what she was?

"Touch me," she begged him, rising on her toes to push her body against his hardened manhood.

He groaned, his hand slipping down her back to cup one cheek of her bottom, wrenching her against him. The action placed her directly over his manhood, long and thick. It teased her through her silk gown.

"I'm going to make you come," he panted against her mouth, working her against him.

She moaned, biting her lip as exquisite pleasure rocked through her core and throughout her body. She helped and moved with him, falling into a rhythm. He sucked in a breath, kissing her, dragging her against him, and playing her like an expert musician.

"What are you doing to me?" she begged, wanting more. They were in a secluded area, hidden by plants, but still, anyone could wander and come across them. That no longer concerned her. All she cared about was what Rowan was doing to her. What he was making her feel.

"The next time I make you come this way, Princess, it'll be with my mouth."

The idea of Rowan kissing her there with his lips and tongue was all it took to send her tumbling over the edge. A conflagration of ecstasy thrummed through her core and out into her body, shattering her to pieces. She worked herself against him, taking from him all that he would give her. Her legs gave way, and he hoisted her harder against him, giving her all that she craved.

"Rowan," she gasped, his kiss silencing her moan. In time the spasms ebbed and slowed and then disappeared altogether, but still, awakening lingered. The realization that there was more between a man and woman than she had ever known.

She could now understand the secret looks and touches shared by her sister and her husband.

How wonderful that a union could be so enjoyable. She wanted the same for herself. And she wanted it with the man in her arms. "I had no idea that such a thing was possible between a couple."

He chuckled, helping her to stand on her own two feet and checking her gown quickly. "There is a lot between a man and woman. That is merely only one."

Excitement thrummed through her veins. She knew she could not experience everything with Rowan. Some lines she could not cross until she was married, but what they had done was nothing so very bad. And no one had to know.

She reached up, running her finger along his lips, reddened by her kisses. "You say the next time you make me come it shall be with your mouth. I look forward to the event," she teased, wishing they could have a repeat of the night already this moment.

He took her finger into his mouth, suckling it. The breath in her lungs seized, and she fought not to faint with want of him.

He pulled her finger free of his mouth, kissing the tip of her finger. "As do I, Your Highness." His deep, gravely voice made her body burn. "The wait will be worth it. I promise you that," he declared before returning her to her party as if he had not changed her life forever after their walk.

CHAPTER 8

*a*lessa was kept busy over the following days with several callers, men who seemed confident enough to request an audience with her. Marco and Rowan always stood close by, and during the several days of gentlemen callers, she had noticed that Rowan's mood had darkened and grown more annoyed with each one.

Was the man jealous? Did he not like seeing the woman he had made shatter so pleasantly into a million pieces be complimented and flirted with by other men?

She could not help but smile at the idea that he did not want her talking to the other men, considering their advances. For all their lovely titles and wealth, they were a fun diversion for a time, but she would never consider any of them.

None of them made her heart beat fast or her skin prickle in awareness. Not like her body did when she was around Rowan. He had not touched her or sought her out during the past several days, but her time had not been her own, and she knew he wanted her all to himself.

She could sense it, feel it each time their paths crossed.

His hands flexed at his sides whenever she walked past. As if he wanted to reach for her, take her in his arms, and kiss her senselessly.

His annoyance toward her gentlemen callers was obvious. Rowan seemed to take pleasure in placing himself about the room in locations that enabled him to intimidate the poor fellows.

She supposed she ought to speak to him and tell him that his actions were unnecessary and not appreciated, but she could not. She liked that he was protective, resentful of those wanting to acquaint themselves with her further.

Perhaps by seeing what he could lose, he would want it for himself.

Today she had risen early and ordered a bath, wanting to have the morning to herself. Aunt Rosemary was out shopping, and the duke was at his club, and so for a few hours at least she had time to herself.

She stepped out of the bath, wrapping a drying cloth about her, and walked into her room. Her maid had stoked the fire high before heading downstairs to press several gowns she wanted to wear this week.

Alessa made a little yelp at the sight of Rowan leaning upon the backboard of her bed, his arms positioned lazily behind his head.

His gaze devoured her, and she quickly strode to the door, snipping the lock before rounding on him. "What are you doing in here?" she whispered. "It is one thing to steal a kiss or two, but you cannot be in my room."

He shrugged, not moving an inch. "I think it's time that I tasted you, Princess. Just as I promised I would."

Her mouth dried at his words. He could not mean what she thought he did. And now? It was the morning.

Servants were about, and her guard Marco was no doubt just out in the passage.

She padded over to him, standing just out of reach. "You must leave before you are caught and sent away. We will not be able to do anything if you're punished for being here."

Without warning, he moved and hauled her onto the bed, settling her atop him. Her traitorous body forgot all the reasons why he needed to leave and purred instead at the feel of him.

She was naked, except for her towel. The fact she recognized on Rowan's face when it hardened, became more determined than ever.

He reached out, removing her hands from where she clasped the towel at her chest, letting it fall away. She sat atop him, as naked as the day she was born. Never in her life had anyone seen her in such a way, but she could feel no fear, no embarrassment. The way Rowan took in her every curve, every part of her, left her warm and achy and utterly wanton.

He shuffled down on the bed, lying flat, and clasped the backs of her thighs. "Climb up on me, Princess. I need to taste you."

She could not do such a thing. It was too much. Not at all ladylike. She bit her lip, debating his words. Her body was aflame, weeping for his touch just as he taunted, and she placed herself above him as he wanted.

Her face burned at the thought of what they were about to do, but her need overrode her embarrassment. He clasped her legs, pulling her onto him and her world tipped. She clasped the headboard, steadying herself as his mouth latched on to her, suckling and teasing.

It was too much. Never had she ever experienced

something so decadent and wicked. She moved atop him, working herself against his eager tongue and lips. As much as she tried, she could not stop his name that fell from her lips. Her body hot and damp, her sex coiled tight. How had she lived without experiencing such exquisite pleasure?

His tongue worked her needy flesh with renewed vigor, and without warning, she was floating, spiraling into an abyss of incandescent delight. Rowan moaned, suckled her harder in one unique place that made her gasp. She threw back her head, riding him, taking all that he offered without fear or embarrassment.

"Rowan," she breathed, slipping from atop him to lay at his side. She met his gaze, his dark with need and satisfaction. "You tempt me more than I should allow." She leaned over, kissing the skin on his chest. He smelled of man, of sex and lavender. Her gaze dipped to the apex of his thighs, not missing the large, solid mass of masculine form that jutted against his breeches. "Would you like me to help you find pleasure too?" she asked him, sliding her hand down over the corded muscles of his stomach to his groin. She took him in hand, rubbing him through the material of his pants.

So large and long, thick too. Would they even fit should she do the unthinkable and lay with him in earnest?

"Not today, Princess. I should leave before I'm caught in your room."

She did not want him to leave. She wanted him to stay, to touch her again and make her feel all that he had before. Their interlude was too quick. Was over too soon. She wanted more.

He moved off the bed, and she leaned up against the headboard, watching him as he righted his rumpled clothing. His dark hair fell a little over his face as he tucked his shirt back into his breeches. The dark shadowing of stubble on his cheeks made him look like a pirate who had stolen into her room

Her lips twitched at the imagining.

"I should not be here," he said, his harsh tone surprising her. "Nothing good can come from our attraction."

A little of the euphoria that surrounded her after their interlude dimmed at his words. "I know," she agreed, hating that for their circumstances, that may very well be true. Her sisters would not like her choice. They would fight her will, should they hear she wanted to marry her guard. But was she reading into what they were doing more than she ought?

There was little doubt in her mind the man before her, his rugged, handsome face, the hardness that all but oozed from him, made him unattainable, not someone, anyone, would look for to marry. But there was also something soft, vulnerable about him when he touched her that she wanted to see more of. Of course, he demanded a response from her, pushed her to be a little wild, but he never forced, was never rough with his demand.

"But I do not want whatever this is between us to end. I'll be here until the end of the Season, and your protection is required until then. Can we not enjoy what time we have left and not worry about what is to come? I'm well aware already of what my life will entail moving forward. What we have is a sweet diversion that I'm selfish enough to want to continue."

He came and stood at the end of the bed, staring at her. His face showed no emotion. He was so very hard to read, and it maddened her that she may never know all of what made him who he was.

He reached out, clasping her ankle, his touch sending goosebumps over her skin before he wrenched her to the end of the bed. She squealed, laughing as he came over her, settling between her legs.

"We can continue on with our little liaisons, Your Highness. I'm here to serve you, after all. But I shall only do so as long as you understand that once you leave England, our association too will come to an end."

Alessa purred at his words, wrapping herself around him and holding him against her. He was hard again, and she ground herself against his sex, wanting all that he offered. And if he agreed to stay now, to continue their little rendezvous, then there was a chance for them—a chance for her to win his heart and trust and make him hers forever.

"That's all I ask," she said, pulling him down for another kiss.

For now.

CHAPTER 9

owan had only just left the princess's
bedchamber when Marco came upon him,
relieving him of his duties to break his fast. As much as he
wanted Alessa in his bed, wanted to lay claim to her, make
her his, he could not allow himself to dream of a future
with the woman.

She was no ordinary woman. She was a royal princess
—a king's daughter and sister to a queen.

Not for him, a street urchin from nobody knows whom.

He stood at the side of the ballroom later that evening.
The *ton* at play, the dancing, laughter, and abundance of
privilege they all lived with made his skin crawl. How he
loathed how much the wealthy had when the poor had so
little. The gap between the two classes growing ever larger,
growing ever harder for those who had nothing to their
name.

Rowan received word today from those who wished to
do Alessa harm, demanding that action be taken sooner
rather than later. The princess was settled in London,
trusted those about her, and it was time to strike.

Tomorrow evening he was rostered off from duties, and he would take care of two more of the henchmen who sought to do her harm.

Piedro and Dino often hung together, slinked around London, taking from those unaware they were about to be mugged, men and woman alike, it did not matter. The fiends had no remorse or empathy for anyone, even people as hard done by as themselves.

That Princess Alessa's uncle had put in place these blackguards before his death told him a lot about the man's character.

You are no better, Rowan. You were one of those men he hired.

He forced the thought from his mind, refusing to allow it to take root, to grow and fester. He was no longer working for them, no matter what they may think on the matter. He now worked in truth for the princess, and he would keep her safe from harm. Keep her alive for as long as she was under his care.

"You are playing a dangerous game, Rowan. I hope you know what you are doing," Marco said, his voice low to ensure privacy from those at the ball.

Rowan fought not to react to the faithful guard's words. Did he mean his knowledge of those who wished to do the princess harm or something else? His stomach lurched. Surely he did not know of his involvement with the princess. They had been so careful not to be caught.

"I do not know what you mean," he said, keeping his voice level.

"I saw you," Marco said, meeting his eye but a moment. "Leaving the princess's chamber. I know what you were doing in there, and I should warn you against it. She will not marry you, or more to the point, men like us. It is not allowed."

His attention snapped back to Alessa, her purple tulle gown accentuating her petite figure, the flare of her hips and legs he knew went on for days. He hated the truth of Marco's words. Why could she not be for him? He knew she was not. Hell, he'd stated the same to her only hours before, but that did not make it any easier to bear.

He wanted her. All of her. The thought of her married to someone else made him want to strangle the life out of every gentleman here.

"There is nothing between us. You are mistaken," he lied, ignoring Marco's mocking laugh at his side.

"I am many things, Rowan, but a fool is not one of them. I know everything that happens to Princess Alessa. It is my job as her main aid to know and keep her safe." Marco sighed. "I do not interfere in her life. She is a princess, and it is not my place to state what I think is right and wrong when it comes to her heart, but take care. Do not think there will be no punishment if she is ruined or your affair is discovered. She will suffer, yes, but you will suffer more."

Rowen heard the warning in Marco's words. Should he continue, he would be punished if any harm, socially or physically, came to the princess. He ought to stay away from her. Let her swains and bucks that flocked to her skirts carry her away into the sunset as she desired. She was in London, after all, to find a husband, all young women of similar age and rank were, but he could not. Even now, watching as the gentleman paid court to her, complimented and preened before the princess set his teeth on edge.

He unfisted his hands at his sides, taking a calming breath.

What Marco said was true. He needed to remove those

who wished her harm and then leave England and never look back. That was what would be best for them all, as hard as that truth would be to follow through with.

"As I said, nothing occurred, Marco. You are mistaken, but I'll be sure next time that we're not seen alone with one another. Like you, I do not want to see the princess harmed in any way."

Marco moved past him like clockwork about to do another sweep of the room. "Just so we understand each other, that is all I wanted to clear up between us."

Rowan understood all too well. He would keep Alessa safe and then watch her leave or marry an Englishman. The notion brought no solace.

He caught Alessa watching them before she bid her many admirers goodbye and started over to him. He could not remove his attention from her person as she gracefully swept through the throng of guests. Her long, golden locks coiled high atop her head, a small diamond tiara set within the curls, making her appear the very princess she was born.

In his imagining, the gown fell away, exposing her perfect form for him to feast on. How was he to keep away from her? Especially when he did not want to.

"You look all pensive and worried, Mr. Oakley. I thought your mood might be brighter after our morning together," she said, her voice light and teasing.

If he had not just promised Marco to keep away from her, he would have had her on her back someplace within these walls, giving and taking pleasure from her wicked self. His selfish wants and needs could harm her, and he did not want that for her.

"Marco suspects that we've been intimate. He's warned me away from you."

She gasped, staring up at him before her gaze swept the room, no doubt looking for her loyal guard. "But we've been so careful. Are you certain that he saw?"

"He mentioned seeing me leave your room this morning. And I believe his words were that although he does not know what occurred in your room, that the door was locked and closed, well, I believe he understands what we were about."

Alessa paled, and he wanted to wrap her in his arms, pull her against his chest and hold her until she was no longer troubled. "What if he should write to my sister? I shall be sent home immediately. I do not want to leave you."

Her words eased his aching soul. How he wished they could remain in their little cocoon of just the two of them. Enjoying each other's company and body whenever they liked.

But like all dreams, they dissipated upon waking up and facing reality—his more stark than hers.

"You must submit to enjoying the Season and those who wish to pay court to you. Forget about me and what we have done. It is of no consequence. You need to treat me like the guard I am and nothing more."

The scent of her perfume, fresh and fruity, teased his senses, and he steeled himself to be strong. To not allow her to throw her life and reputation away on a man who was not worth it. And he was not.

He'd killed others in his life. Had stolen and lied. Hell, he'd been hired to kill her. She deserved so much more than he could ever offer her. He'd been a fool to start anything at all with the princess, no matter how alluring she was.

"You do not mean what you say. Do not be frightened

off by Marco. If he does not write to my sister, which I do not believe he shall when I think upon it, we shall be fine. He is loyal to me. Protects me. He will not expose me to my family."

"That you are fearful of your family knowing of me should be proof enough that I'm no good for you. Our rendezvous must end, and that'll be it. The decision is made."

She scoffed and flounced off in the direction of Lady Bagshaw. He followed her at a more sedate pace, determined to do one right thing once in his life, and leave her the hell alone.

*A*lessa strode into the foyer the following morning, dressed in a carriage gown of teal green, a small, feathered hat atop her head, finishing off her attire. Both Marco and Rowan stood at the staircase banister railing, waiting patiently as ever for her to be ready.

"I'm going out today. I am viewing a property in Fitzrovia that I'm looking to have made into a women's shelter." She continued walking, a footman opening the front door for her. "Mr. Oakley, you can remain here. I shall only need one guard today."

Marco shot Rowan a startled look before clearing his throat. "Your Highness, it is best that we take Mr. Oakley with us. There are rumored threats in London against your person. We need a second guard on the back as well as the front of the carriage to keep you safe."

She sighed, wanting them both to know she was displeased. She was acting a silly little fool, but she could not help herself. Being a princess gave her opportunities that others did not always receive, and if she wanted to use one of those opportunities and be put out by what Rowan had said to her the evening before, then she would.

She heard the hastened footsteps of Aunt Rosemary, who had agreed to go with her, especially since she was hoping to invest in Alessa's women's shelter and help as much as she could.

"I think you are too wonderful to be true. Helping those who are less fortunate than us. I will be sure to mention it at cards with my friends when next we meet and see if they would be willing to invest in your great cause," Aunt Rosemary stated, pulling on her gloves.

"It is the least I can do," she stated, starting for the carriage, her guards flanking her every step.

It wasn't long before they were traveling out of Mayfair and into the less-fortunate areas of the city. The poor living conditions for some of those in London becoming more apparent the farther they traveled from the opulent neighborhood. She hated seeing the poverty and the misery people faced every day. It placed them in vulnerable positions where sometimes they were forced into situations that are not safe or legal.

There was little poverty in Atharia. Her sister the queen had taken great pains in ensuring those who had slipped into poor living conditions under their mad uncle were once again earning a wage and providing for their families.

"As a woman who was in a vulnerable position last year in Atharia, I know how scary it can be to flee when you do not know where is safe. To seek help elsewhere is one of the hardest and scariest decisions I've ever had to face in my life," she stated to Aunt Rosemary, who sat across from her. "My uncle made a fool out of me before the royal court, called me a whore, among other names. If it were not for the few servants who were loyal to me and my sisters, I'm not certain I would have escaped. They saved me that day, for my uncle had taken a terrible dislike to me in particular, and I would not have been surprised had he not had an order put out to have me killed."

Lady Rosemary gasped, the jowls on her cheeks shaking a little at her horror. "Do you believe so? Surely your uncle would not be so cruel or mad."

Alessa turned away from the window, the harsh living conditions that met her eyes depressing her more and more. "I would not be surprised that the rumor of henchmen here in England trying to kill me was true. I know he is dead, but radicals live on with his desire for a king, and no queen in Atharia. I should think my sister has kept the truth from me, but I'm no fool. There is a reason why I have so many guards. Two in particular who hover about me like a shadow."

Aunt Rosemary chuckled, her eyes alight with mirth. "They do indeed do that. I agree with you, but there is little point in your uncle striking at you now. He is dead. There is no one else to take his place."

Alessa sighed. "That is true, but that does not mean they would not hurt us just out of spite. To push their point, their rhetoric that we ought not to have the power we do. To try to take that power away from my sisters and me. My uncle was mad, and he has frenetic followers. I would not put anything past the man."

"Well, at least you are safe here. There have been no attacks, and you're most adored in society. I know several gentlemen who admire you and would be more than willing to marry you if you only looked in their direction. And now, once the *ton* hears of your charitable heart, well, they will be kissing your silk slippers even more than they were before. Eager to help and contribute."

"I do not need them to kiss my slippers, but they're most welcome to throw a few coins my way to help fund my charities." She paused, thinking. "The women's shelter is not the only project I wish to fund. I have an orphanage I'm going to be helping as well. I have so much, while others have so little. I could not live with myself if I did not try to help where I can."

"You are a remarkable, strong, and charitable young woman. I am proud to know you, Your Highness," Aunt Rosemary said, taking Alessa aback, having not expected such praise.

"I do what I can and when I can. We were brought up to be kind and generous. It is not remarkable at all. Merely my duty to try to afford people their basic human rights."

CHAPTER 10

The carriage rolled to a stop, and Alessa looked out the window at a large reddish-brown rectangular-shaped building. The grounds were overgrown with weeds, and the roof looked as if a good wind gust would topple it to the ground.

Marco opened the carriage door, letting down the steps, and she took his hand, climbing down onto an old gravel road filled with ruts and puddles of water. Not only would the building require major repairs, but so too the outlying lands and road.

They walked along a small, grassy path. She was glad she had worn her ankle-high boots today and nothing more delicate to look over the building. A carriage pulled up behind hers, and her secretary jumped out, notebook in hand, before he started over to them all.

"Your Highness, apologies for my lateness. The wheel of the carriage became a little bogged just up the road. Do take care on your return home that you do not suffer the same fate as I almost did."

She nodded before continuing on. "What do we know of the building, Mr. Todd?"

"Well, it was built approximately fifty years ago as a stable for a large estate that has since been torn down. The stable remains, but over the years, everything within its walls has been stripped by locals and looters alike. If you intend to use it as a women's shelter, you will need to rebuild the floors, the second and third story, and then and only then will it be possible to outfit it with all the amenities we've spoken about already."

Alessa came up to a large, wooden double door that stood ajar, allowing the weather and animals free rein to enter the building to cause decay and rot. She had so many plans to help. She wanted at least a hundred beds set up in the home. Large fires to keep the women warm, and lessons to help improve their abilities and their chance of work. No woman would be allowed to leave unless she was gainfully employed.

"You shall find a builder who's willing to take on the job for a fair but reasonable price. Preferably someone local, who knows the people and would be less likely to be targeted for theft and the like while the building is in its construction stage."

"Of course, Your Highness," Mr. Todd agreed, scribbling in his notebook.

"Once the roof is on and the windows and doors repaired, the building should not suffer too much from the elements. But it is certainly the perfect size for my vision. I think this will do very well." She turned, wanting to walk around the outside. "I'm going to venture a little farther. I shall see you when we return to London. Have a name of a builder for me by the end of the week," she requested, starting off along the side of the building.

She felt more than heard the heavy footfalls of Rowan as he came to walk behind her. She tried to ignore the flipping of her stomach at having him so close to her again. Last evening after the ball, she returned home and had suffered a night where he had not sought her out.

Not that she should allow such liberties, but after their interlude the previous morning, she could not help but want more of him. They had not been so intimate that she was placing herself in harm of conceiving a child. The men and women in the court back home were always having love affairs, some of them boldly so. She could not see so much harm in a little flirtation.

It is not just a little flirtation, Alessa.

No, it was not, she supposed. She cared for the man at her back. She wanted to keep him for herself. Not that she would be allowed. Her family would never allow such a union.

"You did not need to accompany me. I did not ask for your company," she said curtly, annoyed at her family more than the man at her back. If only she were from a normal family, her marriage or union or whatever was happening between her and Rowan would not be a factor.

"Well, you have it." His words were as blunt as her own.

She wanted to turn about and face him. Force him to take back what he had said the day before and let them continue with their little romantic interludes whenever they pleased. To tell her that he would fight for them. Ignore anyone who said they would never marry and marry her anyway.

She did not like not getting her way, not when it came to matters of the heart, her heart in particular.

Boldness getting the best of her, she turned just as they

rounded a corner and were out of sight of the others. "I suppose you think I'm splashing about my wealth. Trying to help others is quite high-handed of me. Is that why you talk to me so coldly, Mr. Oakley?" she asked him, hating the idea that she would never kiss him again. Never have her way with him whenever she pleased. Never have a kind word or sweet look that made her weak at the knees ever again.

Because he had decided she was too far above him and he too far beneath her.

He clasped his nape, a pained expression crossing his handsome face. "I do not think that at all. I think what you're doing here is simply wonderful. I'm honored to serve you and all that you stand for."

Alessa could not think of anything to say to such words. She did not want him to serve her like a good little servant. She wanted him, the man. She wanted him to be beside her when she made such decisions and worked on such charities.

"Well, that is pleasing to hear," she said, at last, wishing he would state he was wrong the other night and did want to be part of her life. Help her in all her endeavors, both here in England and Atharia.

Alessa realized that here at the end of the building, they were quite alone. She wanted him to close the space between them and kiss her already. Instead, he remained apart, arms behind his back, head high and proud. Determined to keep her at arm's length.

She moved off, wanting to see the other side of the building. "Did you have an easy childhood, Rowan? Sometimes I think that you did not."

There was a hardness to him and coldness too sometimes. He was a man who seemed to protect himself by keeping others away. Was that what he was doing to her with his pushing her away? Abiding by Marco's advice and ending them before they had a chance to begin? She did not want anything to end between them. She wanted to live, to enjoy life to the fullest. How could she do that with a husband who alighted no fire in her belly, no matter how *suitable* he may be.

Last year she had stared down a bleak future, one where others tried to tear her down, take her life in fact. She would no longer live in fear, and neither should Rowan.

"My childhood was very different to yours, Your Highness. That is all you need to know about my life."

She glanced at him and noted the muscle in his jaw flexing, his body all but vibrating with unease. Did the memory of his childhood anger him? Hurt him? Scare him in some way? Whatever happened that could cause such a response?

Nothing good, her mind warned.

"I'm sorry if it was hard, Rowan," she said truthfully. Hating the idea that he was poorly treated or ever hungry or cold. Everything she wanted to stop for others if she could help it. Even in this small way. "I'm trying to help the women of London who have no place to go, no future or hope, but I have not forgotten the children."

"You intend to help children as well?" he asked her, the interest in his tone palatable.

"I do. There is an orphanage I'm to visit next week. Will you come with me? I can always use an opinion from those who have not had abundance and safety their whole life. I would welcome any suggestions that you may have, both for here and the orphanage rebuild and restructure."

He stared at her, and she could see he was trying to see if she was being honest or merely teasing him.

"I'm in earnest, Rowan," she added. "I so often have people who do what I say, no matter if the idea is worthy of proceeding with or not. No one naysays me. If you could give me opinions, not be afraid to hurt my pride, I think that would only be beneficial to those who will benefit from my charity."

A small smile turned up his lips, and her heart gave a little thump in her chest that he was honored by her request. Of course, she meant what she said, but she would also welcome the fact he would be around her a lot of the time to give opinions.

He did not want to continue their little affair, but that did not mean she could not make his distancing from her hard. In time, hopefully, when he was beyond his endurance of doing the right thing, he would come back to her, and she would be waiting for him when he did.

She pushed on through the long grass, the hem of her gown sodden. Perhaps she ought to find more projects to do if only to keep him all the closer.

*O*n the journey back to Mayfair, Rowan sat at the back of the carriage with another guard, Malcolm he thought his name was. A beefy Scotsman who often sat behind the princess should anyone try to shoot her from behind. The Scotsman would take the hit before the princess inside the carriage.

He should have studied this job before taking it on. Had he known Princess Alessa had a heart of gold, he would never have accepted the assignment. Tonight he was off, and he would remove Piedro and Dino, who he'd seen on several occasions lurking about the park across from the London townhouse.

They were waiting, watching, and set to strike when the opportunity arose. But they would not succeed. After this evening, they would both be more corpses floating in the Thames.

He found them several hours later outside a tavern that was nestled against the Thames shoreline. The stench of rotting food thrown into the waterway making his eyes water as he strode up to the building.

Laughter and male voices floated across the air. Piedro and Dino would be here this evening. Their particular lady friend sold her services at this tavern every Thursday evening, and they were never not part of the clientele each week.

He entered the building, moving like a ghost through the crowd. He did not stand out, an outsider who did not belong, for he did belong with these people. In his life, he had been as poor as those who drank their worries away or rutted in the darkened corners like animals. He drank the stale beer like everyone else and ate the stew that often repeated on him the next day.

No one took any heed of his being there, and he settled himself at the end of the bar, ordering a beer from a bar wench with breasts that almost spilled from her tattered gown.

This was the reason he had taken the job to rid the royal princess from the world. He did not want this life. It rotted a person's soul, made them hard and cruel. He, too, had once been so—a man without honor or reflection.

Until he'd met Alessa and she had shown him that there was good in the world. That some people of wealth were trying to close the gap between the two societal levels and make it better for those less fortunate.

He knew she would not succeed. In the years ahead, long after he was dead, there would still be poverty, people who stole and killed like him to survive. That the rich would get richer and the poor poorer.

No princess from Atharia would change that fact.

Piedro and Dino stumbled into the bar. Both of them shouting out for their particular whore. Rowan watched as Piedro slunk away into an adjoining room to the bar to have his way with the woman who presented herself.

Dino sat a few chairs from Rowan, unaware of his presence and gulping down his beer as if he had not partaken in a dozen already that night. His unfocused, bloodshot eyes were proof enough that tonight's murder would take little effort.

Rowan sipped his beer, waiting for his moment to strike. He was a patient man, and he could wait all night.

CHAPTER 11

*A*lessa should not be where she was, but neither could she not have followed Rowan to find out where he was this evening. She sat in a hackney cab, having paid the driver a hefty sum and one of her guards, not Marco, to stand watch and shoot anyone who threatened them.

She wore one of her maid's gowns and no jewels, even though she had been at a ducal ball earlier this evening and had looked as regal as her sister the queen.

As much as she loved her life and all that was afforded to her due to her station, she would like nothing more than to settle in the country in Atharia. To raise babies and keep her little family all to herself as much as she could. Her sister was queen. She was more than capable of ruling the country without her help.

She kept her eyes peeled on the tavern that Rowan had entered. Her heart lurching into an uneven rhythm when her guard's flintlock clicked somewhere outside, his low, rumbling words moving a local along who stopped to gawk.

She supposed they did not get many carriages in this part of town, certainly not ones that stayed at least. Dread curdled in her stomach that Rowan may too become suspicious of the carriage and find her out. Would he be mad?

Oh yes, he would be furious that she had put her life at risk simply because she needed to know what he was about and what he was doing. If she was down here in this part of town, it was his fault. She could blame all of this on him if she thought about it.

Voices carried from the tavern door, The Wet Magpie. She sighed, not wanting to know how that name came about when two drunken men stumbled out onto the street, a large woman and man holding a batten, threatening them to not come back until they could pay.

Her heart went out to them. The poor men really did look down on their luck, what with their tattered clothing and unwashed appearance. She had brought her purse. Maybe she should give them some money to help.

Alessa debated this a moment before another man came out from the tavern. Something about the way he held himself, melding into the background and yet present, was familiar. He shifted into the shadows, and she lost sight of him, but she knew he was still there, somewhere.

Was it Rowan? Why would he be following the two unfortunates?

The two men stumbled out onto the laneway before their heads tipped toward her carriage, their interest piqued. She bit her lip, wondering why they would come toward the vehicle, with no hesitation in their steps.

Her guard warned them off, but they ignored him, continuing on.

"Aye, look what we have here," one of them said.

The click of the flintlock halted their steps, but they

were close enough now that she could make out their faces. They were scarred, dirty, and so unfortunate-looking that Alessa did not know whether to feel sorry for them or afraid.

One of the men smacked the other in the chest. "Aye, that's the princess. What's she doing ere?" he said, grinning and showing a mouthful of rotten teeth.

"Making our life easier, that's what," the other stated, reaching down his side to where a large, glittering knife appeared.

"Stand down, or you'll breathe your last," her guard declared, his voice brooking no argument.

One of the men, the shortest of the two, rubbed his stubbled jaw. "I think we'll take our chances. You only have one flintlock. One shot at a time."

"And you only have one knife," a voice came from the shadows, dark and deadly in its warning. Alessa gasped, having not seen the man follow the others. He was like a ghost that haunted the London streets, a shadow that slinked and stalked people unaware.

She shivered at the thought before a blade flew through the air, lodging with a sickening thud in one of the men's neck. A hand shot out, and another knife, one she had not seen the stranger holding at all, found its mark in the other man's chest.

Neither unfortunate men made a sound, nor did they have time to react. Alessa slapped a hand over her mouth, forcing herself not to scream.

"Go home, Your Highness. This is no place for you."

She gasped, looking past the two dead men on the road to the other who stepped into the light.

Rowan!

Her mind reeled at the thought that Rowan had

murdered two people without a flicker of doubt or remorse. She stared at the men, bleeding their lifeblood away on the cobbled road, and couldn't quite fathom what had happened.

"Go," she ordered, sitting back on the squabs and forcing her heart back into her chest. What had happened? Had Rowan killed two men? Of course, she knew that it was a possibility that all her guards at some point in their lives had killed another human being, but to see it acted out, so cold and calculating, was another thing entirely.

Somehow she had placed Rowan on a pedestal above such actions, and she wasn't certain she was comfortable knowing he should not be up there.

They arrived back in Mayfair a short time later. Alessa directed her guard to sneak her back into the house via the servants' entrance. She made it to her room without Marco seeing her. A feat if ever there was one, for the man missed nothing when it came to her welfare.

She bathed and climbed into bed. Tonight she had followed Rowan to see what he was about, where he was going, and what he was doing while away from his duties here. What had transpired was not what she had thought to see.

She blamed it on a woman's vanity, needing to know if he was entertaining himself in the seedy taverns in London and with the women who plied their trade within their walls. She had not expected to see what she did.

Her mind, tired from thinking over the evening events, gave her rest, and she dozed on and off during the night. Her dreams, horrible and violent, were full of blood, faceless foes chasing her along the darkened alleys of London. Chilled air kissed her skin, and she gasped, sitting up when she spied a man at her bedside. A hand shot out and covered her mouth, muffling her scream.

"Shush, Alessa. It is me. Rowan," he said, slowly removing the pressure on her lips so she could speak again.

What would she say to him? What would she demand of him? She wanted to know everything. Why he had gone to the tavern in the first place and why he killed those men and not simply knocked them out cold. They did not deserve to die. Knowing who she was as they did, was no reason for them to receive a death sentence.

She stared at him, uncertain how to word the question she had to ask. In the end, she decided directly was best. "How could you have killed those two men this evening? Was such force necessary?"

The bed dipped as he sat beside her, and she moved back against the headboard, needing space.

"They would have raped and killed you, Alessa. Forgive me my actions, but I would never allow that to happen to you."

She stared at him, so matter-of-fact and unbothered by what had happened. She could not be so calm.

"What did you do with them? Did you leave them there? Did you bury them?" Her mind fought to understand what had occurred.

"Threw them in the Thames where they belong. Rubbish that can float out with the tide."

She felt her mouth gape before she snapped it closed. "They would not have hurt me. I was well-guarded. They merely needed money that I could have given them. Given them a chance at a better life."

He chuckled, but there was no mirth in the gesture. "They knew who you were, and they would have killed you. Why do you think I was there tonight? For the entertainment, or hearty food at The Wet Magpie?"

Alessa had been asking herself that question too the entire evening, why he was there and with whom. "Tell me then, so I do not think you a cold-blooded killer without a heart."

*B*ut that was the crux of his life. He was a cold-hearted killer without a heart. One hired to infiltrate her world to gain access to her, so she too could be killed by his hand.

He was a bastard to his very core.

"They were under instruction to kill you. There is an active threat against you in England, and they were paid to have you eliminated. You walked straight into their world and offered yourself up like a cherry on a cake. They would have killed you and thought nothing of it after the fact."

She shivered before him, and he reached down, pulling the blankets up about her waist. He ignored the sweet scent of apples that teased his senses or the fact that her breasts were all but visible from the moonlight spilling into the room. "And you knew this, and that is why you were there? To keep me safe?"

Well, he was keeping her safe now, but there had been a time when he had been one of those men, so desperate for money that he had no honor, no heart left to care.

A time before Alessa.

"I knew of their plot and had planned on killing them before your inappropriate arrival. No one saw anything, being as late as it was, and I doubt anyone would care if they did. The two men were not well-liked. Trouble and strife some called them."

Alessa reached out and placed her hand atop his. "You were there, putting your own life at risk to keep mine safe?" Her tone warmed, and some of the fear dissipated from her eyes. "I owe you an apology then. I'm sorry I followed you and that I inadvertently placed myself at more risk. I shall not do so again."

He shook his head, guilt curdling his blood. "You do not owe me an apology for anything. I'm glad that you are well, and nothing happened to you before I came outdoors." When he'd seen her in the carriage, her eyes wide and frightened at the accosting from the two men, he'd almost swallowed his tongue.

That she thought herself in the wrong made him wince. He was the one in the wrong. No matter that he was trying to right that error now, it did not change the fact that he had set out to murder an innocent woman.

How could he have agreed to such a job? Knowing Alessa as he did now, he knew he could have killed a woman who called to his own heart.

"You're a good man, Rowan. I'm lucky that you are part of my security here in England." She bit her lip, a small frown between her brows. "Would you consider coming back to Atharia with me and continuing your services there? I know I would not like to lose you."

Oh, how she tempted him, but he could not. He could not remain her guard and watch her marry and have children with another. Torture on the rack would be less painful than that.

"I'm to America when you return to Atharia, Your Highness," he said, reminding her of who she was and he was not. "I intend to make a new life there, far from England and the darkness that plagues this city."

Disappointment shadowed her eyes, but he could not relent, not even to please her. Their interlude here was as fleeting as time. She would marry someone suitable and powerful to keep her safe, and he would sail away and never look back.

CHAPTER 12

*A*lessa wasn't sure how to change Rowan's mind. If he were to travel to America, he would be so many miles away. She would never see him again. She reached out, cupping his cheek, the stubble on his jaw tickling her palm. He leaned into her touch, and her heart stuttered in her chest.

"What if I do not want to marry a prince?" she whispered. "What if I told you that my life has been full of enlightenment and fun, spontaneity and pleasure since I met you. How can I return to Atharia and marry a stodgy old prince after knowing you?"

"What of Lord Douglas? Was he not near to proposing to you last year in Atharia? He follows you about at balls and parties, hell," Rowan said, running a hand through his hair and leaving it on end. "All the men follow you about, and they should be the ones you allow to court you. Not some nobody from the slums of London. A man who hasn't a penny to his name. I have nothing to offer you. I may give you pleasure and snippets of excitement, but I cannot give you a future, Alessa. I can give you nothing."

How she hated to hear him speak in such a way as if there was no hope for them. No future. She was a princess. She had power. Her sister was a queen. If she wanted to marry a man who had no monetary value, then she would, for to her, he was priceless in so many other ways. He was the sweetest, most loyal, and honest man she knew. And he made her stomach flutter each time she looked upon him. How could she not care for him?

"I do not want anything from you but you, Rowan. Is that not enough?"

He cringed and went to stand, but she grabbed his arm, stilling him. "Please do not leave. I want you to stay."

He shook his head, standing. "You do not know what you ask. You do not know what kind of man I am. If you did, you would never give me a chance." Rowan pulled away and started for the door, and something in his tone, the devastation, the warning, halted her need to go after him. She would give him this night, but that was all. Tomorrow she would fight for him. Make him see that there was a future for them if only he were brave enough to reach for it.

"You do not get to make my decision for me, Rowan. What I do and what I want in life is for me to decide. That applies to whom I care for and whom I do not. I do not care for the swains who waltz and bow before me at all the balls and parties. I only care about one man who stands at my back and guards me against harm. I will not cower or apologize for what I feel for you, no matter how much you may think yourself unworthy or do not feel the same for me."

He flinched at her words, the knuckles on his hand gripping the door handle turning white. "I'm sorry, Your Highness, but I cannot give you what you want." He stormed from the room, careless as to who may be outside her door, keeping guard.

No sounds or raised voices came from the hall, and she could only suppose he had chosen an opportune time to steal into her room and exit again, possibly when Marco was checking the exterior or grabbing a bite to eat, which often helped him keep awake at this late hour.

She slid down into the bedding, pulling up the blankets, and stared at the wall. Whatever was she going to do with Rowan? He was so very determined to keep her at arm's length. And that would never do.

She did not want to stay away from him. She could talk her sisters around to adoring him as much as she did. She was sure of it. As for Rowan, well, he may take a little more persuasion, but she had all Season, and that had only just begun.

*A*lessa stood at the side of the Earl of Lytton's ballroom floor and ground her teeth. Marco stood behind her, but another guard, not Rowan, stood alongside him. For the past week, she had not seen Rowan and had vague, indifferent answers to her queries from Marco that annoyed her to no end.

She refused to dance with anyone who asked her. Her mood had been sour, and there was little point in pretending to be otherwise.

"My dear, you're scowling at everyone," Aunt Rose-mary said at her side, procuring two glasses of Ratafia from a passing footman. "Whatever is the matter, my dear?"

Alessa debated telling her ladyship of her troubles but then thought better of it. She would definitely tell the duke, and then she would be on the first ship home to Atharia.

"I think I am getting my courses. I feel very put out and upset," she lied, facing her ladyship. "Would you mind if I returned home? With my guards accompanying me, you are more than welcome to stay and enjoy what's left of the ball."

Aunt Rosemary looked about, debating her words. "If you're sure, Your Highness. I do not mind cutting the night short and returning with you if you prefer."

Alessa reached out, taking her hand. "No, you stay and enjoy the ball. I shall retire for the night. I think that is what I need."

What she really needed to do was find out where Rowan was and demand to know how he could just up and leave her without a goodbye at the very least.

After all they had done together, how could he treat her so coldly? How could he think it was suitable to treat a woman in such a way? Alessa downed the sweet beverage and handed the glass back to Marco to deal with. "I shall see you in the morning, my lady."

Her ladyship smiled, and Alessa started off toward the doors, her guards fast on her heels. Now all she needed to do was figure out how to escape their notice, too, so she could find Rowan and ask him what he was up to.

The fiend would not get away with treating her so deplorably.

The ass.

*R*owan lay on the cot in his small room rented from a widow of a merchant in Spitalsfield. The sounds of the city, of the people plying their nightly trades, the drunken racket of men who walked from tavern to tavern halted any sleep he was trying to gain.

The scent of damp and the pungent fellow who lived downstairs wafted into his room. He had asked for time away, had not explained to Marco why he needed to step back, but something about the other guard's willingness told him he understood his troubles.

Some of them, at least.

The words that Alessa had said to him not a week before ran through his mind. She had wanted him and no one else. That she thought him honorable and kind. Honest!

What a farce that all was. He was none of those things. He was a killer, plain and simple. His soul was cursed, and she deserved so much more than he could ever give her. He could not allow her to change his mind, to let him consider they could have a future. They did not, and he would be a fool to believe otherwise.

She would have no future at all had he done what he was hired to do. Had he completed the job and killed her when he had the chance, there would never be a future even to imagine.

She deserved to know the truth. To know everything that he had done in his life. The many murders, bribes, fights, and deals he'd made. Including the one against her. How could he allow someone so pure, sweet, and innocent to even be within a foot of him?

He ought to be hanged for his crimes, not admired by the woman whom he had sworn to kill.

A knock sounded on his door, rapid and hard. He jumped from the bed, ready to give whomever it was that interrupted his mental anguish a fist to the nose.

He wrenched the door open, ready to do exactly that,

before the breath in his lungs expelled. He glanced up and down the corridor, pulling Alessa into his room before shutting the door just as quickly. He thrust the bolt across the door, locking them in and turned to face her.

She was pale and breathing heavy, the black hood she wore of such a high quality, he couldn't help but wonder how she had not been mugged and stolen of it.

"What are you doing here? How did you even find me?" he demanded, holding her shoulders and shaking her a little as if that would give him the answer any quicker.

"I stole into Marco's office after a ball this evening, and he had your address listed in his ledger for wages. I wrote it down when he was relieving himself," she said, her voice calm and matter-of-fact.

She pulled out of his hold, slipping the cloak off her hair and gifting him with the view of her long, golden locks. They were pinned up as if she were still attending a party or ball. When she slipped the cloak off altogether, the golden silk gown coming into view, he knew she had come from an evening out—another night where men fell at her feet and worshipped her. The types of nights he could never offer her, no matter how much he wished he could.

"You are lucky to survive coming here dressed like that. That gown alone could feed a family for months. Some would have stripped you bare and left you naked and alone in the street without a care. Do you know that?" he asked her, his tone harsh and critical.

He hated admonishing her, but she needed to know she could not chase him down in this part of the city and think it was all well and safe. It was not. Men like him lurked the streets, and she did not want to run into the likes of him out there.

"I have a gun, Rowan. No one was going to hurt me, and I've paid the hackney well. He is waiting for me outside."

Rowan walked to the window and wrenched up the pane, shaking his head at the street below where no hackney cab waited. "Really, Your Highness? Where is your carriage?"

She tsked tsked and came to stand beside him, looking out on the street. Her mouth opened on a disgruntled puff, and some of his anger dissipated. But not by much.

"What if you had the wrong address? What if what I had told Marco had been incorrect?" Which it had been, and that Marco knew his true location was a failure he would have to remedy, and fast.

Should Marco find out the truth of his being near the princess yet again, he was as good as dead, no matter if Alessa vouched for his life.

"I suppose I would have been in trouble then, but you are here, and everything is well. No need to get so irritated with me, Rowan. It is I who is angry at you and not the other way around."

He crossed his arms over his chest, raising his brow. "Really. Do enlighten me, Your Highness, why I am out of favor."

She copied his stance, and he felt the utter fool holding on to the position he stood. Even so, he continued to stare her down, wanting to know how he was at fault for trying to do the right thing.

He had never tried to do the right thing by anyone until Alessa. She ought to be proud of him. If she knew the truth, that was.

CHAPTER 13

"*B*ecause you are obstinate and argumentative, simply because you are poor and I am rich. That is what it comes down to, does it not? You think I'm above you, and you are beneath me. But you're mistaken, Rowan."

He failed to see how he was wrong about those facts. They were as clear as night and day, and she was fooling herself if she thought they did not matter. "Again, enlighten me, Your Highness."

She sauntered up to him, raising her chin. He had the overwhelming urge to kiss her puckered lips and wipe that smug look off her face. Instead, he steeled himself to listen.

"I am more than what I was born, just as you are. We are not just products of our upbringing and surroundings, our haves and have-nots. I am a person under all the sparkle, the diamonds, and silks. Why can you not admire me for me and forget about everything else that surrounds us?"

What she asked was impossible, but goddamn, so very tempting. He did want her. He did not want to share her with anyone, not now or ever. But how could they have all that they wanted? It was impossible and not fair for either of them to dream such things when they were not plausible.

Rowan reached out and clasped her cheeks. Her eyes all but begged him to see her, the real her. And he did see the Alessa beneath all the sparkle, as she called it. He had recognized some time ago the good, honest heart that beat in her chest. The kindness she exuded to those around her, wealthy and poor alike.

"I do see you, Alessa. Never doubt that I do, but wanting something does not make it possible. You must see that."

Her hands came up to settle on his chest, and he felt his blood quicken. They were alone here. No one knew where she was, and they would certainly not expect her to be with him. Spitalsfield, in particular, was no place for a princess. It was no place for anyone, really.

She shook her head. "I do not see that at all," she said, obstinate to the very end. "Now kiss me, you infuriating man before I expire from waiting."

He needed no further urging, no matter how much he wished their time could last forever. That them being together wasn't merely a dream, but a reality. But it was not. They were worlds apart, and he would lose her. It was only a matter of time.

He fought to do what was right. To not allow her to hope for more. To not allow himself the same, but as she stared up at him, the need that radiated from her, he could not deny her anything. He had wanted to kiss her the moment she had entered his room, and he fell into that want without remorse. He took her mouth in a searing kiss, warmth and need exploding through him like never before.

She welcomed his kiss, her hands fisting the material of his shirt. He knew he looked poor. He was living in reduced circumstances compared to her. This room, sparsely furnished and with the pitiful fire burning in the grate, was no place for Alessa to be. No place for him to make love to her.

But he would. The selfish side of him taking what she offered even though he knew it was wrong. He would have this night, give her this one memory and then never touch her again.

He scooped her up into his arms, carrying her the two steps to his bed before lowering her. The mattress was lumpy and old, and he cringed.

Stop, Rowan. This doesn't seem right.

She frowned up at him, a question in her pretty blue eyes. "I do not care about the bed, about the room, anything. I only care about you. You are who I want. I would not be here if that were not the truth."

Her words went some way in soothing his guilt, but not all the way. Rowan kissed her again, taking his time to savor the sweet taste of her lips, the glide of her tongue that maddened him. His cock hardened, and he ached to have her, to make her his. To have the one thing that no one else ever would have.

Her innocence. If he were so fortunate, her heart as well.

"Undress me," she gasped, breaking the kiss. "I want to feel you. All of you."

He kneeled between her legs, helping her to sit up and discard her heavy cloak. Her gown had numerous buttons running along her spine, and it took more time to free her of it. She grinned when it finally gaped at the front, and she was able to shuffle out of it.

Rowan ripped his shirt from his breeches, tossing it to

the floor without care. She sat before him in nothing but her shift and silk stockings.

The skin on her calf to her thigh was so soft, unmarred by a hard life. He played with the small, pink ribbon that held it in place, ticking her flesh with it. "I do adore these silk stockings. And upon your legs, they're a work of art," he teased.

She lay back on the bed, leaning upon her elbows. "How fortunate of me to find a man who appreciates a ladies unmentionables." Her lips twisted into a mischievous grin, and he chuckled.

"Hmm, I think I shall leave them where they are." Her eyes widened in awareness. Rowan untied the little ribbon at the front of her shift before pulling that, too, free from her person and discarding it on the floor.

He swallowed, reveling at the sight that she made, so pure and perfect. Not a blemish marred her skin. She was the epitome of privilege, but right now, she was also his. He could not believe the woman in his bed wanted him. He was a nobody with nothing to offer, and yet, there she sat, her eyes heavy with desire and need.

He licked his lips, the corset pushing up her breasts, making him ache. He wanted to strip her naked, but the sight of her, a siren in his bed, overrode his need.

She lay down, beckoning him with her arms, and he lowered himself upon her. Her legs cradled his ass, pulling him against her. Rowan groaned, rocking into her quickening flesh. She bit her lip, sighing in agreement. He'd never heard a more erotic sound in his life.

He reached between them, ripping his front falls open and pushing down his breeches. His cock sprung free, and he guided it against her wet, glistening mons. She felt so good, so wet and ready for him.

"Promise me you will never hurt me, Rowan," she asked him, clasping his face in her hands.

He nodded, steeling himself to take his time, to never hurt her, not here or in the future. Not unless it was for her own good and safety. "I promise, Alessa."

She arched her back, placing him at her entrance, and the temptation was too much. He thrust into her, taking her and making her his. Taking her innocence and what ought to be a gift to her future husband.

A little sense of pride, of glee, ran through him that he had been the first man the princess had ever been with and wanted in this way. A man so far beneath her he ought not to even wipe her boots, nevertheless have her as a bedmate. He was a dangerous man, untrustworthy and mean, and created by the people who made up his horrific childhood and adolescence.

Alessa should not have him anywhere near her person, and yet she did and never had he ever felt more complete than he did right at this moment.

*A*lessa stilled at the stinging pain that caught her unawares. She had wanted Rowan so much, had ached for him so much that the uncomfortable feeling assailing her was a bit of a shock.

He leaned down, kissing with slow, tempting strokes against her lips. "The pain will only last but a moment. Try and relax," he urged, not moving and letting her adjust to his size.

And what a size he was. She felt overly full as if they did not fit, and yet, there was a glimmer of pleasure there too. A secret she was yet to realize that tempted her to relax and trust in his words.

She had already experienced incandescent ecstasy without intercourse, but there had to be something else that she was to find out. Men and women were made for such acts. Alessa dedicated herself to do as he suggested, and within a few moments, she no longer felt so at sea.

She pulled him down for a kiss, reveled in the feel of his lips, his tongue, his need of her that she felt with every caress, every touch and stroke. He pushed into her, and she sighed, understanding what it was that left women delirious for their husbands night after night.

Her sister had been one of them, and now Alessa too. She would never be the same again. Not now that she understood what she could have, what Rowan could give her whenever she wanted.

However, would she ever live without him as he wished?

She could not. She had to have him come with her to Atharia. There was no choice but for them to marry and do this exquisite joining every night for the rest of their lives.

Alessa wrapped her legs about his back, taking him deeper. He understood her need and increased his pace, his lips hard and demanding, and she decided she liked that he was a little rough about the edges. He had always been honest, told her his thoughts and opinions without the fear of hurting her feelings.

Everyone walked about her as if they were walking on fragile ice, and she hated it. No one was honest. No one was themselves. With Rowan, he had always been the opposite, and she adored that about him.

It was why she trusted him now with this, the ultimate act of trust.

She kissed him back, wrapping her arms around his

shoulders. He thrust into her with delicious strokes that teased and taunted her to madness.

Her blood felt aflame. Her nipples ached and puckered hard against her corset. He teased her with each stroke, and she could not get enough. She took all that he gave, the need, the feeling of completeness overwhelming her, building within her body like a kaleidoscope of feelings.

She thrust up against him, needing more, wanting him harder, faster. To take her and not care about the consequences. He understood her silent plea and thrust harder, faster, and then she was floating into an abyss of pleasure that was too much and yet never enough.

"Rowan," she gasped, her climax muffled by his kiss. He took her with a madness that threw her into more delicious spasms. She held on to him, both of them entwined as one as he found his own pleasure with her.

For several minutes they lay entangled. His warm breath kissed her neck with each exhale before he slumped to the side, pulling her up into the crook of his arm. She snuggled into him, placing a small kiss on his muscular chest.

"I thought when we had been alone before that nothing could surpass what you gave me, but tonight, well…" she said, a silly grin lifting her lips. "Tonight was simply enlightening. I had no idea such pleasure was possible."

He stared down at her, a lazy smile upon his lips. He looked relaxed and happy, more so than she had ever seen him before. A little feminine pride roared through her that she had done that to him. A woman of no sexual prowess had made him succumb to such heights.

"It has never been this way for me either, Alessa, if that

is what you wanted to know. You are a remarkable woman, and I adore you."

His words, sweet—and something told her truthful to the very core of them—left her discombobulated. She had not expected such endearments, but she adored him too, loved that he was different. That what they had was unconventional, complex, and wonderful.

It gave her hope for them. That perhaps she could persuade him to fight for her, not be so quick to walk away just because their social standings were so vastly diverse.

They were more than what they were born.

"Tell me tomorrow you will be standing behind me once again at balls and parties. I have missed you so very much with you being away."

He leaned down and kissed her, rolling her onto her back. "I'll be by your side, Princess. I promise."

Alessa smiled. "Good, I'm well-satisfied then," she said, spiking her fingers into his hair and pulling him down for another kiss. And another after that.

CHAPTER 14

*A*lessa felt like a new woman. A woman who had a delicious secret and one that made each day brighter and more exciting than they ever had been before in her life.

Tonight, they were to attend a musical evening held by the Dowager Countess Howe, one of Aunt Rosemary's friends. The evening would conclude with a light supper and drinks.

As promised, Rowan had remained by her side these past days, and when she could, she had caught snippets of time to be alone with him, but only fleeting.

It was not enough. She wanted more moments together, but how to gain them when Marco had become increasingly observant, not to mention present most of the time?

Alessa sat before her dressing table mirror and watched as her maid pinned up the last of her hair, the string of diamonds carefully woven in afterward to finish her dressing.

A knock sounded on her door, and she bade them

entry. The breath in her lungs seized at who stood on the threshold.

Her sister.

The queen.

Alessa schooled her features to one of pleasure, for she was happy to see Holly, but could not figure out what on earth she was doing here in England. Panic seized her that something had happened to their younger sister Elena.

"Your Majesty," she said, standing and dipping into a deep curtsy. "Whatever are you doing here? Is Elena well?"

Her sister nodded, smiling. "Elena is very well," she said, walking over to her and bussing her cheeks before pulling her into a quick embrace.

"I'm so happy to see you, Holly. It has been months and months." But now that she knew Elena was well, she could not help but wonder why Holly had traveled to England. Had Marco written to her? Impossible. She would not have received a letter so soon. She had to be here on another matter of business.

"I am pleased to see you too, Alessa. We have missed you back home. But I do not bring good news, unfortunately. And I do believe it will stop you from being able to see out your Season here in London."

Alessa felt the blood drain from her face. "Whyever not? What has happened?" she asked, slumping back onto her dressing table stool.

"If you'll excuse us," her sister said to her maid. "Please bring up a fresh pot of tea. Thank you."

The maid dipped into a curtsy and left, closing the door softly behind her.

"Why can I not stay?" Alessa asked again. She had not had long enough with Rowan to convince him to remain at her side. To fight for a future together, to marry her if he would have her.

Holly sat in one of the chairs before the fire, and Alessa joined her. Something about her sister's demeanor, the seriousness of her tone putting her on edge. Something was very wrong and bad enough that her sister had crossed an ocean to fetch her back home.

"It is by chance that I'm here in London. Drew needed to return to England to settle some things relating to Sotherton Estate, and so we thought to spend some weeks in London with you. A surprise, as it were. But upon arrival, Marco handed me the latest correspondence to be sent to Atharia and informed me that there is a bounty upon your head. That to strike at me and the crown of Atharia, a gang of thugs wishes to harm you."

"Who would do such a thing?" Alessa asked. There were always threats against all of them. They had grown up living with vague reports of people wanting to do them harm, and they had learned to live with such threats. She knew coming to England, there were rumors of men loyal to her deceased uncle's plans who did not want her here. Her many guards were proof enough of those threats, even though they had done nothing to strike at her yet.

"Our uncle may be alive, Alessa, and still playing his deceitful games. It is said he's here in London and has had men at the ready to strike at you. Have you noticed anything peculiar of late? The feeling that you are being watched or targeted?"

She frowned. That could not be true. "But he died. We buried him. You sat with him as he took his last breaths."

Holly shook her head, seemingly as confused as Alessa was at this news. "I received word from him that he played us all the fool. That he did not die, merely staged his death.

I do not know if this is true or not, but it is said he is here in England, hiding in the bowels of London, waiting to hit out at us as soon as he can.

Alessa's mind whirred at the news. There were always people who did not believe in monarchy, but to want her death was not something she had imagined at all.

"I cannot believe our uncle is alive, but of course, if it is true, then that changes my level of safety here in England. I know he will not stop until he gains what little advantage he can. Injuring me, killing me, will hurt you. That is enough for him."

"It is worse, Alessa, and please, do not become hysterical when I inform you of what I know."

Alessa steeled herself to hear whatever else there was to know about this threat. The only comforting element of her predicament was that Rowan was by her side. He was protecting her from those threats and keeping her safe.

He really was her own knight keeping his lady safe.

"Marco suspects that the security hired for your duration of stay in London has been compromised. That someone who is working for the Crown of Atharia, is in fact, under contract to murder you."

A cold shiver ran down her spine at the thought. She clasped her forehead, feeling a little dizzy at the idea of such a thing. All this time and people around her could have done her harm?

Surely not. All her guards had been caring, loyal, and above reproach.

Rowan has not always been so loyal, a small warning voice whispered in her ear. When she had first met him, he had been prickly and cold. But that did not make him a murderer.

She thrust the doubt aside. Rowan had grown closer to

her because of their mutual feelings for each other. Not because he wished to kill her.

A man who made love to a woman as he had made love to her was not a murderer—a cold-hearted bastard paid to do others' dirty work.

"I do not believe it. It cannot be true," she said, her body revolting at the idea. "I trust the men around me. They would not do this. Your sources must be wrong."

"We have brought guards from Atharia to continue to secure us all and to keep a close watch on those already in service. If there is any doubt raised on any of them, we will know of it soon enough. But you must not tell anyone, just in case it alerts the guard we're trying to catch, and they flee."

Alessa nodded. "Of course. I will not say a word." Not even to Rowan. She would not disobey her queen or her sister on this.

She supposed this was not the time to tell Holly of her feelings for Rowan or what they had been about these past weeks. This new dilemma would muddle everything. Make it that much harder to explain or gain acceptance from her sister about the man she cared for above anyone else.

"I'm to visit an orphanage tomorrow in Seven Dials. Will this still be agreeable, do you think? I shall have the extra guards, but I cannot stop living my life. I must go on and do what I can for those less fortunate than us, even if others are out to strike us down."

Holly pursed her lips in thought. "I think it shall be acceptable, but we shall take a carriage without the family crest, and we shall take a route that isn't common, just in case our plans were leaked. I think that is best, but we can no longer stay for the Season. Drew's business will take a month at most, and then we shall return to Atharia, where I know I can keep you safe."

"But I have just started working on getting my women's shelter started. We haven't even started the renovations there yet. And as for the orphanage, my secretary is still trying to source the owner so we may purchase the building." Not to mention the thought of leaving England and never seeing Rowan again was like a physical blow to her chest.

Her sister threw her a consoling look, and the little hope she had been holding on to, to be able to stay, fled. Her sister would not allow it, and she would not go against her queen. Not regarding her safety, at least. Holly had never led Alessa or Elena wrong.

"I'm sorry, Alessa, but you'll have to put in place here before we depart a person of business to oversee all the building works, at least until we have our uncle and his men under control and dealt with. I will not lose you or Elena to these thugs."

"Very well," Alessa said, hating the idea of leaving England and Rowan, who had already declared he would not follow her. Why though? Why could she not get through to him? Make him come with her, be with her forever.

"That is not the only reason I wanted to speak with you," Holly said, pinning her with a determined look that put Alessa on guard.

A shiver of unease ran up her spine, and she could not help but think whatever else they needed to discuss would not be an as easy conversation, as their last had not been. "What else did you want to address?" she asked, keeping her tone level and unperturbed.

"Marco tells me that you've formed a close friendship with Mr. Rowan Oakley, one of your guards. Is this true?"

Oh dear, so Marco had told her sister. Granted, he had waited for her to arrive in England, but still, this was a delicate matter, and she had hoped to have more time to work out every particular of their relationship so she could explain it better to her sister. Hopefully, in turn, gain her approval and acceptance of Rowan.

"We are friends, yes. I did not think that was against the rules. Perhaps Marco has forgotten his place," she added a little more tartly than Marco deserved. Of course he was concerned, he knew the rules just as well as Alessa did, and he knew when one of his men was crossing the line.

But what about her? She had crossed the line just as eagerly as Rowan had, and that could not all be laid at Rowan's door.

"Now, now, Alessa, no one is accusing you of anything inappropriate yet," her sister added. "But you have never formed such a close bond with any of your guards in the past, so it is odd that you have done so now. As it is, I thought to return to London to hear of your betrothal to Lord Douglas. Are you no longer interested in that gentleman? Has he injured you in some way?"

So many questions. Alessa took a calming breath, deciding to answer her sister's second query first. "Lord Douglas is a friend and will remain so, even if he does seek out your approval for our marriage. I do not feel romantically inclined toward him, and that is the end of it. I wish him very well in his future."

Holly raised her brow, watching her keenly. "And Mr. Oakley? Do you feel romantically inclined toward him?"

Heat rushed to her cheeks, and her sister sighed,

reading her like a book. "Alessa, please tell me you have not fallen in love with your guard. You know I can never condone such a union. He's a servant. You're a princess. A marriage between you cannot occur, no matter how much you both may wish it."

Alessa knew this, of course, but hearing it made the horror of being separated from Rowan forever all the harder to bear. She could not do it, so the rules had to change. Her family's expectations had to alter to accommodate her feelings that were growing stronger and stronger every day toward Rowan.

"I will not give him up, Holly. No matter what you or anyone else says. Not if there is a future between us. He is the only man whom I've ever had any emotional sway toward. He makes me laugh and smile, and he protects me from harm. How could I not love such a man?"

"Very easily because you are not allowed to, Alessa. Why would you act on such feelings? Are you sure you're not merely swept up in his sweet words that you've never had said to you before? We all have lived a very cossetted life. You may be confused."

Alessa shook her head, knowing she was not confused at all. She saw everything very clearly now. "I'm not confused. I know what I want, and it's Rowan."

CHAPTER 15

*T*hankfully they were interrupted by a knock on the door. Alessa bade her maid enter and was informed that the carriage had arrived for their evening out. Her sister clasped her arm when she went to leave, wanting out of the room and away from the awkward conversation.

"We have not finished discussing this subject, Alessa. We shall address this matter further after you've returned from the orphanage tomorrow morning." Her sister stood back, letting go of her arm. "I hope you have a pleasant evening."

Alessa wasn't sure how pleasant it would be now that her sister had told her she could not marry Rowan. Not that Rowan had made any advances toward marriage, but one did not lay with and love as much as he had her and not want a future.

"I will discuss the matter with you then. Good evening," she said, walking from the room, glad to be going out after all, even if it were only a musical night.

The night passed pleasantly enough, although the

abundance of guards outside the Dowager Countess Howe's home and near her person inside was obvious and, in truth, not sustainable. She would have to leave if only to be able to walk about without so many eyes upon her every moment of her life.

She did not see Rowan that evening, and she slept badly, nightmares and cold sweats keeping her awake. All too soon, it was morning, and she was downstairs, preparing for her meeting at the orphanage when her private secretary knocked on the library door.

"Good morning, Your Highness. Let us go over this morning's appointment if you're willing?"

"Of course," she said, gesturing for him to sit. "Tell me how the day will play out, if you will."

Her secretary studied his notebook. "You shall meet with the headmistress of the orphanage at first, and then you shall do a walkabout, meet the children, watch them in their classes before you bestow on them your donation."

Alessa turned, happy to be talking and thinking about anything but what her sister had stated the night before. That she could also see Rowan walking about in the gardens, keeping watch, was a second distraction she did not need. To see what one could not have was never pleasant.

"My plans have changed, Mr Todd and you will need to hire a competent manager to overlook both the orphanage and women's shelter's refurbishment and construction."

Her secretary looked up, adjusting his spectacles on his nose. "You're leaving, Princess Alessa?"

She nodded, the pit of her stomach churning at the thought. "I am, and so regarding the orphanage, I will need assurances and updates that each child will be fitted correctly for new shoes for summer, including clothing for both school and play. We're to repeat the gift during the winter months, and I want the finest wool used for their winter cloaks. They must be kept warm and dry. I insist upon it."

"Of course, Your Highness," her secretary assured, jotting down numerous notes. "And I can hire a competent manager. Both the orphanage and shelter will be a testament to your kindness and an asset for those who seek help."

"I hope so," Alessa stated, watching Rowan speak quickly with Marco. She hated that she could not go and seek him out. Talk with him, touch and kiss him as much as she would like.

"Do you still intend to dine with the orphans at lunch?" her secretary asked, pulling her from her thoughts.

She nodded, looking forward to meeting the children and giving them a little treat at meeting a princess. She hoped that her trip would educate and provide the children with the belief that people did care about them and their futures. That they could be whatever they wished should they attend to their studies and work hard.

"Of course. Why wouldn't I?"

Her secretary glanced down at his notes, a light blush stealing over his cheeks. She narrowed her eyes. "Is there a reason I would not be so charitable to these children? Is there something you wish to say to me?" she pushed him, wanting to know if anyone thought her too regal to be so charitable.

"Well..." He coughed, clearing his throat. "It's just unheard of that a princess, a sister to a queen, would dine with those so beneath her status. I merely want to ensure you are making the correct choice for both yourself and the crown you represent."

Alessa ground her teeth, having not known her secretary held such arrogant, highhanded opinions of her and such low ones regarding children without a family. "I will be dining there," she said, her tone clipped and brooking no argument. "That will be all. Thank you, Mr. Todd," she said, ending the conversation. She took a calming breath, knowing she would come up against such opinions every day should she pursue Rowan. Their gazes met through the window, and she smiled. He grinned back, and she knew she could not give him up, no matter what anyone said or their opinions on the matter. She would fight for him, and she would get her way. She was a princess, after all. No one said no to her, and nor would Rowan.

A short time later, they arrived at the orphanage in Sevan Dials, making the premises just before lunch as planned. Alessa stepped from the carriage, Marco and Rowan at her sides as she took in the sight that beheld her.

Children had lined up on either side of the stairs leading into the building, holding little paper flags of her homeland. The sight brought tears to her eyes, and she spent several minutes talking to them all, thanking them for such a lovely welcome to their home.

They followed her indoors. The headmistress, a woman who looked to be in her thirties, came forward, dipping into a deep curtsy. The children behind Alessa chuckled at the sight of their teacher showing respect, and she smiled. "Miss Winters, I presume?" Alessa stated, reaching out to shake the woman's hand. "How lovely to meet you at last."

"Oh no, Your Highness, it is all of us who are blessed by your presence here today and your patronage. We cannot express how privileged you make us all feel, knowing we have your support."

Alessa looked back at the children, their little faces making her heart ache for the trials in their life up to now. How could so many be without family, without love? She hoped they were all happy here and well-fed and cared for. Her tour today would ensure they were and that care continued well into the future, but with a building fit for purpose.

"It is I who is honored. I'm happy to be here, meeting you all and supporting the children on their journeys to adulthood. While my time here in England may be short, my support of this orphanage will be lifelong. I promise you that."

The young headmistress fumbled for a handkerchief, dabbing at her eyes. "You are truly a gift from the angels, Your Highness. Please," she gestured into a nearby room where Alessa could see a tea tray and some biscuits awaited them, "come through into the sitting room. The children have a special performance arranged for you to watch if you're willing."

Alessa started toward the room. "I am very willing indeed. Let us begin, shall we?"

"Indeed," Miss Winters stated, rallying the children for the short concert.

Alessa smiled, enjoying her time at the orphanage, knowing that with her privilege, she would make a difference to these children's lives and those still yet to walk through the doors.

CHAPTER 16

$\mathcal{S}$he settled on the only cushioned chair in the sitting room. The other teachers were a little shocked at her presence, but welcoming nonetheless. Alessa was used to this kind of attention, and while when she was within the *ton*, it was displayed less than with the general populace, it was still a condition of her birthright that she had come to accept as normal and commonplace.

She was a princess, had abundant wealth and privilege, but she could not keep it all for herself. Her uncle had been greedy, had tried to steal what was not his, have everything for himself and nothing for anyone else. Not even the people of Atharia.

Alessa and her sisters were not so inclined. However, her being here today, her monetary support, and her presence would help this orphanage give every child a better start in life. Help them to succeed so they could break the poor, undereducated cycle they had been born into.

The performance was a little play about friendship, how to help others when alone and scared. A positive message to those watching that she knew had been written

115

to represent what she was doing for them. Their gratitude, their sweet little smiles as they took their bows, was the best gift she had ever received in her life.

Alessa stood, clapping. "Thank you all so much. What a wonderful group of children you are. I enjoyed the performance very much."

The headmistress looked like she was going to burst with pride. "There is a special lunch in the hall, children. I hope you enjoy what Princess Alessa has organized for you all today."

The children squealed and ran from the room, some tripping over in their haste to leave. The headmistress turned to Alessa. "We shall dine on a table in the hall with the children, if that is suitable, Your Highness. We can discuss any concerns or suggestions for your charity during our meal or in my office afterward. The children will be so distracted by the feast that I do not think they will be overly concerned about what we speak," she suggested.

Alessa followed the headmistresses out into the hall, which too needed repair. Old, faded wallpaper had started to peel from the wall, the floor requiring several new boards as some appeared rotten. Multiple windows had little bolts of cloth pushed into holes to stop drafts. She sat in a chair at a small table that had been covered in a white cloth, but even Alessa could see the table leg had once been broken, and the chairs they sat upon did not look sturdy enough to hold anyone upright for long.

"Again, Your Highness, we cannot express our gratitude enough for you being here. We have tried for several years to gain a patron or patroness willing to help us keep the children schooled and clothed. It is very hard, as a lot have been surrendered to us permanently from their families, and the ones who stay but pay tuition, pay very little.

We barely make enough to keep coal in the two fires we do use during winter."

Alessa looked about the room and caught Rowan watching her, his visage one of adoration and wonder. Had he been a child without a family? A young boy cold on the streets of London without food or care? She closed her eyes a moment, hating the thought of it, wishing she could save everyone who faced such a bleak life.

Alessa turned back to Miss Winters and gave her her full attention. "This whole building is in need of repair from what I have viewed of it so far. I know I promised to clothe the children each year until they are employed and earning a wage, but I want to do more."

Miss Winters pulled out her handkerchief once again and dabbed at her nose, her eyes wide with hope. "More, Your Highness? You are already doing so much."

Alessa did not think so. She had more money than she knew what to do with. When she died, she could not take it with her, so why not spend it on children while she could? The children here deserved it just as much as any other child, after all. "I am going to have repairs undertaken on the orphanage, Miss Winters. The entire building shall be purchased from whomever you lease from to ensure its location and safety in the years to come. I would never begin repairs only to have the landlord turn about and kick you all out and make a profit of my charity." Alessa turned to her secretary, who stood nearby. "Mr. Todd, ensure the deeds are transferred over to my trust before the end of the week. Pay whatever the value is for this part of London and add a little extra to smooth the sale."

Mr. Todd nodded, jotting down in his notebook. "Consider it done, Your Highness.

"I will have every room repaired, lined, and heated for

the winter months. No longer shall the children here go cold, which I understand has been a concern for you."

Miss Winters nodded. "In winter we have to have all the children housed in the same room at night. Coal is expensive, and I can only afford to have two fires lit, you see, and so with the children all together, the room is warmer. Not a lot, mind you. We lost a child last year to a terrible chest infection. I believe if the building were heated better, we should not have lost Gregory."

Alessa frowned, hating the idea of a child dying, no matter what the circumstances. "I'm sorry I did not know of your plight sooner, Miss Winters. Losing a child would be traumatic, and you cannot blame yourself. You are trying to help these children, care for and love them as best you can. It is not your fault you do not have the financial means to continue."

Miss Winters nodded, but the poor woman clearly blamed herself for the child's death. Alessa reached out, patting her hand. "We shall work together to ensure that no child will ever befall such circumstances while under this roof. They all shall be snug in beds that have an abundance of blankets, their clothes will be warm, and their shoes new. The building shall be like a palace when I'm through with the renovations. You should not know yourself after the fact. And," she said, thanking the stars for her blessed life that she could be so generous to those less fortunate, "I shall have every room that houses a fire supplied with wood and coal, so much so that you shall not know what to do with it all. As patron of your orphanage, I will make certain that you, Miss Winters will want for nothing ever again. I promise you that."

"Your Highness, that is too much. We cannot take so much from you," Miss Winters argued, looking at Alessa's guards and secretary for support and receiving none. Marco merely smiled, and her secretary noted everything that was being said down in his notebook.

Her attention snapped to Rowan, who was looking out the window, a muscle working on his jaw.

Alessa turned back to Miss Winters and smiled. "It is not too much at all. I should also like to help hire more staff for you. Another cook and cleaner I think you shall need. And also a person who may be able to source some of the children out for adoption. Those who long for a family and have none of their own. But it must be their choice if they're old enough to decide. Would that be helpful, Miss Winters?"

The headmistress broke down in tears, and Alessa sat back, pouring herself and the young headmistress some tea as she waited for her to regain her composure. Her declaration was quite shocking, she supposed, and exciting. It was a lot for anyone to take in and accept as truth.

She spent the afternoon in the hall with the children, eating some of the roast lunch she had delivered to the orphanage. The dessert was lemon meringue pie, a favorite of Alessa's, and the children, having never had it before, oohed and ahhed as the sweet dessert touched their tongues.

The afternoon passed in a haze of laughter, of small talk, and tours of the building. Alessa could see everything that needed repairs, and it would take several months, but they must be ready before the first snowfall of the season. The building had to be warm for them this winter. That was not negotiable, and she would ensure whatever builder they hired for the position could hit that deadline.

She returned home later that afternoon, not looking forward to her upcoming discussion with her sister. She did not want to argue with Holly. She wanted to sit in the library and design and plan the repairs at the orphanage, make a list of items to discuss with the headmistress when she met with her again next week.

Alessa stepped from the carriage and stumbled as a crack sounded out in the street. A puff of dust flew up from the step she was about to step upon before she gasped as a body hurled against her, pushing her onto the cobbled footpath, her chin hitting the pavement and making her teeth clatter.

"Stay down," she was demanded. Alessa did as she was told, the realization of what had just occurred spinning through her mind.

She heard footsteps and shouting and lay still as she could before she was hoisted up into the arms of Rowan and rushed into the house.

He set her down inside the hall, slamming the door closed behind them.

"Did someone just shoot at me?" she asked him, unable to believe that someone would dare to do that, but knowing all the while that she was a target and, of course, she was fair game to be felled.

Rowan strode to the window, looking out onto the street behind heavy velvet curtains, careful not to move them or be seen. "Yes, Your Highness. You were shot at, and lucky for you, you're not dead."

Harsh, but true, she supposed. She watched him a moment before she turned and started up the stairs to her room. She wanted to run to him, to wrap herself into the safety of his arms, but he was distracted, looking out onto the street. Her guard in every sense of the word and no longer her lover. Not right now, at least.

"Thank you for saving me," she whispered, glad her tone was calm while the blood in her veins pumped fast.

Rowan met her eyes, a tortured look to his visage. Other servants stood about, all wondering what had happened, what was happening. "Do not thank me. Never thank me," he stated, striding to the front door, wrenching it open, and marching out into the daylight, heedless of the danger that lurked outdoors.

She started as the door slammed shut, putting an end to their conversation. Alessa turned for her room, wondering why Rowan was acting so odd. Why did he not want her to thank him? Of course she was thankful, and would always be so.

Footsteps sounded upstairs, and she watched as her sister ran toward her. Holly wrenched her into her arms before escorting her to her room. What would this new attack mean for her? What it would mean for both of them, she did not know, but she did know her life just became a lot more complicated and problematic. That was one certainty she could not ignore.

CHAPTER 17

The following morning Alessa sat in the library with her private secretary, her sister, and two guards as she listened to them debrief her on what had occurred the day before. Who they suspected and what happened following the shooting.

Marco had been unsuccessful in capturing the wannabe killer, but he had seen him jump up into a highly polished carriage of considerable expense, so the man had money or was backed by someone who did.

Her uncle had been rich aside from his links to the Atharia royal family. They suspected he was working with several allies here in England who disliked that her sister had inherited the throne.

It was only logical that her uncle's spineless friends had made their first strike against her, and she would be a fool indeed to ignore the warning. But she had not long been in England. To leave now would mean they had won, scared her away. She would not back down to anyone, least of all an enemy who did not have the stomach to face her head-on.

"We must depart England immediately, Alessa," her sister stated, striding back and forth behind the desk Alessa sat before. Her sister's husband, Lord Balhannah, nodded in agreement before the fire.

"I agree," Marco stated. Alessa fought not to sigh at her guard's words. Of course he would agree with Holly. He would never not agree with her sister. "It is all we can do to ensure your safety. The next time they strike at you, you may not be as lucky as you were yesterday."

Her guard was right, of course, but the stubborn part of her soul refused to accept defeat. Her uncle had lost the war in Atharia. If he were indeed alive, the man and his absurd supporters needed to stop with this foolishness, especially when her uncle was never in line for the throne, not after his brother, her father had heirs to succeed him.

"Surely we can stay a few more weeks at least, Your Majesty," she begged her elder sister. "With the extra security you have put in place, and if I promise to limit my outings and not let it be known what events I shall attend, that will surely keep me safe until we depart." She did not want to leave, certainly not so soon. She caught Rowan's gaze and read the troubling thoughts, the concern his dark-blue orbs held for her safety. She was not ready to leave him yet, if ever. What if she could not persuade him to come with her? To love her as she had started to suspect herself of loving him.

"If it is true that our uncle is alive," she continued, "can we not at least try to track him down? Bring him to justice here in England and be done with him and his thugs. Should they be caught, we will not have such urgency to leave."

"What makes you believe they are supporters of your uncle? Could they not be Englishmen who dislike foreign rulers in England?" Rowan asked, the first time he had spoken since she watched him storm out of the house yesterday afternoon.

"But we are not ruling anyone, Mr. Oakley. My sister is having a Season like so many other debutantes, and nothing more," Holly stated, a warning in her tone. "She poses no threat to anyone. If anything, she has been a blessing to the people of the city who are so much more unfortunate than us."

"I concur," Marco said, leaning forward on his chair. "I believe it is your uncle's men who are behind this attack. We shall hunt them down, torture the truth from them if need be, and remove all of them from your path, Your Highness."

Alessa rubbed her temples, an ache settling at either side of her head.

"I shall have my secretary inform the Bow Street Runners we require assistance in bringing our uncle to heel," Holly stated. "If he is alive and found, a lovely little boat ride to New South Wales may be just the thing he requires to learn his lesson to not strike out against us."

"Perhaps you ought to take up the invitation from King George to relocate to Buckingham House, Holly," Lord Balhannah said.

Alessa turned to look at her sister, not having heard that King George was privy to their situation and had extended an invitation to them all.

"We shall have to. I will not risk my sister's life," Holly said, reaching out and clasping her shoulder quickly before she started to pace once again.

"Buckingham House?" Rowan blurted, his eyes wide with shock.

"We may be located now at Duke Sotherton's home,

my husband's father's townhouse, but we are royal, Mr. Oakley. The king is a distant relative of ours, and I would expect nothing less than an invitation from him when we are being attacked," Holly stated coldly. Alessa could not understand her sister's dislike of Rowan, but it was clear as the daylight trying to come through the drawn-closed heavy velvet curtains that she did not like him.

Alessa wanted to go to Rowan and reassure him she was still the woman he had held in his arms and made passionate love to only a few days ago. That who they were and related to did not change who she was. He was floundering with the knowledge of who she was and what was happening around them. She inwardly cringed, knowing that this realization would only make it harder for them to be together. He would see her position as a pedestal that he could not reach or ever be able to climb.

She sighed, wishing for the first time in her life that she was just a woman and he was just a man and there was no impediment to their life together.

"We can always transport you to any entertainments you wish to attend from the mews. The garden is not overlooked, and with it adequately guarded, you should be safe to leave from that location," Marco said, meeting each of their eyes.

"I think that would be best, although I think you really ought to limit your outings, Alessa. Until we have those wishing you harm under guard at Newgate," Holly said, her eyes narrowing on Rowan.

Alessa leaned back in her chair. What was wrong with her sister that she did not like Rowan? It made no sense at all.

"I think it wise for you to leave England immediately," Marco said. "But the choice is not mine to make."

"No, it is mine. This is my life, and I will not be bullied and scared back to Atharia like a child." Alessa stood, taking her sister's hands. "You did not cower to our uncle. You fought him, stormed our home, and took it back. There are people here in England who are relying on me. I cannot let them down. I will not. I want to stay," she continued, squeezing her sister's hands a little. "Let me at least secure someone to take over my women's shelter and orphanage, allow me to attend a few more balls, and then I shall return home. I promise you I will not try to dissuade you a second time."

"You may never have the opportunity to return home or talk to your sister again if you have a bullet through your head," Rowan stated, matter-of-fact.

Alessa felt her mouth gape, and she shut it with a snap. Rowan was supposed to be on her side. He wasn't supposed to want her to leave. Did he not want her to stay?

She had spent so much time locked away last year in Atharia. On the run from her deranged uncle, that the last place she thought anyone would strike at her was England. That she would ever be unsafe here.

Why could they not leave her alone? Allow her to live for a change. Her uncle had lost. It was time he gave up the fight should he be behind all their troubles and still alive as they suspected.

"You may be right, Mr. Oakley. These thugs may kill me, but then as a member of a royal family, that is the risk I take every day whenever I step outside and into public life. But I refuse to live my life as a prisoner due to my privileged birth. I have too many things to do, people to help. If I cower and run away, they have won, and I refuse to allow ruffians such as they are to run me out of town just yet."

Rowan's lips twitched, and he leaned back in his chair, his breeches pulling tight across his lap and gifting her the sight of his impressive manhood. She looked down at her hands, at anywhere other than all his glorious form. And before her sister, no less, who was acting odd already around her guard.

She looked up from inspecting her fingers and found him watching her. Her cheeks warmed, and for a moment, she was transported back to his lodgings in Spitalsfield and the bed he'd made achingly wicked love to her.

"We can only guide, Your Majesty, Princess Alessa. The choice to stay or go remains with you," Rowan stated, standing and going to the window. He pulled back the curtain and glanced out onto the street before closing it again. "You will need to keep the curtains closed at all times unless you prefer to use the rooms at the back of the house more than the front. We do not know where they will attempt to strike next. For you to remain here and have freedom as much as you can, I think these protocols will need to be in place."

So, in essence, she would be living as a captive here in London as well. She had spent so much time last year running, hiding, trying not to die before her sister arrived that she no longer wanted to live that way. She was indeed putting her life at risk and those of her guards, but she could not hide away forever. She could not let her uncle win in this way too.

"The bastard," she murmured under her breath. "I agree to leave and return to the house via the mews. I will also keep the front window curtains drawn, but that is all. I will attend the select few balls I have already notified my attendance at, and I shall enjoy them. My position in life will always come with a level of risk that I'm willing to assume. I trust in your protection and that you shall bring to heel those who seek to harm me. The extra protection my sister has brought from Atharia I trust will keep me safe." Alessa met her sister's gaze, reading the uncertainty in her eyes. "Are you in agreement, Holly?" she asked her, hoping she was.

At last, the queen nodded, relenting. "We leave in four weeks, no more. Ensure that all your business is attended to by then. Our departure will not be delayed."

"Thank you," Alessa said, bussing her sister's cheek. "I will ensure everything is in order as required."

Her sister and her husband left and headed upstairs. Marco, too, walked from the room and exited the house via the front door. Everyone but Rowan left her alone.

Alessa studied him, his determined, harsh profile as he stood at the door. Her guard once more fascinated her. She could not help but wonder if he had a family, loved ones who worried about him. Or did he have no one and nothing who would mourn his loss should his position in her household bring him harm.

Alessa picked up her quill, tapping it against the desk. Her fingers stilled when he turned and entered the room, closing the door behind him.

"Have you always been a protector of others, Rowan?" she asked him.

A muscle worked on his jaw before he spoke. "I have been a hired guard for some years now, but it was not always so."

"Do you worry that you could die working for me? I'm not so certain that I could give up my life for another unless I loved them."

He shook his head, his low chuckle mocking. "I have no one who would miss me, Alessa. My only care now is keeping you from harm. If I'm killed, and you are not, my bones will lay easy in the ground knowing I did my duty. Did one thing right in my life."

Alessa narrowed her eyes, watching him as he moved about the room, checking behind doors and furniture that no one was hiding behind. Her lips twitched. "I do not want you to die, Rowan. I would miss you."

His steps faltered. "You should not. I'm a waste of such emotions. Should you know me long enough, you will come to realize that too."

She hated hearing him speak so and she stood, coming around the desk. She wrapped her arms around his waist, holding him close. "You are not a waste of emotions to me. No matter how much you try to dissuade me from liking you, Mr. Oakley, I, for some reason, like you very much indeed." Alessa grinned up at him and was pleased to see a small smile lifted his lips.

"Very much, hey?" he stated, pulling her close. He dipped his head and kissed her quickly. Alessa leaned into him, wanting so much more than a quick, chaste kiss.

She nodded. "And I would like to know everything there is to know about you before I leave. If I'm to persuade you to come with me, I shall need to know everything, so I may use my womanly wiles to get my way."

A shadow of sadness entered his eyes, and then he blinked, and it was gone. "To know me would mean that I would lose you all the sooner. I shall not let that happen."

"There is nothing that I could learn about you that would make me question what I feel for you. If you haven't already guessed, I'm not like other women, Rowan," she stated, meaning every word.

He groaned, wrenching her closer still. "I know that

very well already," he stated, setting his chin on the top of her head.

Alessa smiled against his chest, but there was something in his tone that gave her pause. There was a finality to his words, disappointment that it meant they could never be because she was different. Alessa pushed the depressing thought aside and instead rallied herself to enjoy her few final weeks in England with Rowan. The man she knew to the very core she was falling in love with, and wanted for herself forever.

CHAPTER 18

𝓡owan thankfully had disengaged himself from Alessa when Marco came into the room, declaring a shift change. He bowed before her, wishing he could kiss her goodbye before he strode from the library and headed out the front door. But he could not. Alessa wasn't his to hold and love in that way, in front of anyone who happened by, no matter how much he may wish it were so.

It would never be so, and he needed to remember that fact, even when she held him close and settled against his chest, fitting him like a glove.

She was a princess. He was her guard, a poor, untitled nobody. They could never be together.

The attack against her had rattled his nerves, and he was determined to end this madness against Alessa tonight. The gunshot could have killed her had the assailant had better aim.

The thought of her dead, cold on the street, her lifeblood draining from her body, left him chilled. Rowan walked several blocks away from Duke Sotherton's townhouse before catching a Hackney cab. Rowan looked out the carriage window, spying the Aldgate pump. He was close to the Hoop and Grapes tavern and where he would end the madness against Alessa once and for all.

The carriage pulled to a stop, the windows of the inn illuminated with light and laughter. He entered the crooked door, walking along the wood-paneled corridor before heading out to a back room where Roberto housed his office and underhanded business.

Two men stood at the door, the last two fiends he would have to kill along with Roberto. They did not speak, merely glared, but opened the door, allowing him to enter.

Rowan walked into the dark office. It stunk of unwashed man and tallow. His eyes watered at the stench. He leaned over the desk, staring down at the man who had hired him to kill Alessa. "What was with the attempt against Princess Alessa yesterday? That was not part of the plan, to kill her in the street like some stray dog. I was hired to kill her, not one of your thugs outside the door," he said, gesturing toward where the two men stood outside.

The gentleman, not much older than Rowan, chuck-led, the sound menacing. He appeared the same. With his shaved head and long beard, he did not look like a man to cross. But then, neither was Rowan, and looks could sometimes be deceiving.

"We will strike at Her Highness whenever and in whatever way we can. You have failed so far to complete your orders. Which, need I remind you, you are to be paid handsomely for."

"You led me to believe that the princess and her family were not loyal, kind, or generous to their people. That their hold on the crown of Atharia was illegal. That is not the case. I do not take kindly being lied to, need I remind *you*," he stated, leaning over the table.

The two guards at the door stepped into the room. Rowan hated lies above all things, so to kill because of one was not what he would ever knowingly do.

He was a killer, could kill and be killed at any time, but his victims in the past had their deaths coming to them. Had deserved to die due to their crimes against innocent people. But the princess was nothing like those men. She was honest, so very kind, and sweet to those less fortunate. And as for her charity, he had never seen another give as much as she was about to. To build a women's shelter and refurbish an orphanage, well, he had never seen anyone in the *ton* be so generous. She was a marvel, an angel, and he would not kill her, not for all the money in London.

He was an orphan, a homeless street urchin at the mercy of those around him. He prayed as a boy that someone would save him from the nightmare he lived every day. The nights filled with terror and days of biting hunger. The bitter cold that ate into your bones and made them ache. He could not kill a woman who would be the savior for so many like him who had nothing and no one.

Roberto smirked. "I do not like my authority or my reasons questioned. Are you still with us, or will you, too, be on my list the moment you walk out the door?"

"The princess is nothing as you described. Why kill her? It makes no sense."

"Because she deserves to die, just as her sisters do. They thought to steal the crown from their uncle with no repercussions. They were foolish to think that was the case."

"He's dead, and you cannot become king. What is the point of all of this? You know I only kill those who deserve to meet their maker. The princess does not fall into that category, and I do not like to be used."

"Are you declaring that we're now enemies?" Roberto asked, his tone as cold as ice.

Rowan narrowed his eyes. The two guns pointed at his back, the only reason he stopped himself from reaching across the desk and strangling the bastard. "As of this moment, our deal is over. I will not kill an innocent, no matter what false opinion of her you hold or how much money you offer me."

"Then we will be enemies, and I would advise you not to make an adversary of me, Rowan Oakley."

"I would suggest you not make one of me, and do not threaten me again. You're in my city now, Roberto, not some small Mediterranean island where you have allies and friends. You do not have them here, but I do. Leave the princess alone, or you will die should she be injured."

Rowan stormed from the building, expecting a bullet to lodge in his back as he strode past the two guards, but none came. He used the same cab to return as close to Mayfair as he could, using the time in the carriage to think.

He had made an enemy tonight, but he would strike first and his mark would be accurate. Roberto Delenzo would not live for much longer, nor his two guards. Rowan rubbed a hand over his jaw, wishing he could inform the Bow Street Runners the Queen of Atharia had hired what he knew. Where Roberto ran his business from, but to do so would declare his own hand in this underhanded, honorless deed.

He could not do it. To tell Alessa the truth would mean he would lose her. Mayhap not by death, but certainly because she would hate him once she knew who she had allowed into her home.

Into her heart.

*A*lessa started awake in the library chair when the door to the room slammed shut. Panic seized her that she had been shot at once again before the sight of Rowan tumbling into the room and sliding across the Aubusson rug met her eyes.

He came to rest a foot from her chair, not moving, merely groaning. Alessa leaned over, taking in his appearance and the distinct scent of beer wafting from him. "Rowan? Are you well?" she asked him, knowing that he was not at all well. He looked foxed for certain, but why he was drunk, she did not know, and that worried her more, for it was so unlike him.

"Rowan." She tried again to revive him. "Are you alive or dead?"

His hand reached up, wrapping about her ankle, pinning her to the spot. A shiver stole up her leg and through her body. His warm hand glided upon her calf, massaging and flexing against her flesh.

Alessa closed her eyes, swallowing the ache that his touch wrought within her. He rolled over, his glazed, unfocused eyes warmed at the sight of her. His lips twitched into a lazy smile, one that she had never seen before, and something inside her melted.

How handsome and adorable was this man, even now, in his current condition.

"Ah, my beautiful Alessa. Do you know how difficult it will be keeping you alive and out of harm's way?"

Alessa kneeled beside him, tapping his face and trying to sober him up before Marco returned from patroling the outdoors.

"Rowan, you must get up." She leaned down, and the whiff of strong spirits assailed her. "How much have you had to drink tonight?" she asked, not expecting to receive an answer.

His hand shot out, clasping her nape. He pulled her close, so close that she could feel the warmth of his breath against her lips.

"Enough to know that I should not kiss you, but I will. Even with the threat of Marco and your other guards who could catch us at any moment."

The idea of him kissing her sent a thrill to her core. She wanted him to kiss her, here and now, and bedamned the consequences. What did it matter if Marco caught them? He would not say anything, or at least he might tell her sister, but she certainly would not say a word due to protecting her from gossip.

Her lips twitched when Rowan closed his eyes, seemingly forgetting to kiss her as he promised. *You need sleep. That is what you need, my darling*, she uttered in her mind. She clasped his face, feeling the stubble on his jaw, taking a moment to admire the sharp angles of his face, his dark hair, and lips that made her mad with want.

He was so handsome but still such an unknown to her. She wished he would tell her of his past, of his childhood, but he never did. Was it happy as her own had been, or bad?

Alessa leaned down, kissing his lips, wishing and hoping it had been a good one, unable and not wanting to imagine he had suffered and had no one to guard and love him as he deserved.

Swift footsteps sounded out in the foyer, and Alessa and Rowan stood, moving to opposite sides of the room just as

Duke Sotherton entered. His mottled red face and wrinkled brow told her something was wrong.

"Your Highness, it is Marco. He has been attacked in the backyard and is unconscious. I have had him moved to an upstairs room, and the doctor has been sent for, but I do not think he will survive. It is bad, Princess."

Alessa was already running as the duke spoke the words. Marco could not be injured. He was her rock. He'd been with the family since he was a young man and his father before him. She could not lose him, not when there were those who wished her harm.

She made the room just as a maid broke down in tears, the cloth that she held to Marco's head soaked with blood. The large, jagged cut across his head and down his neck telling Alessa all that she needed to know. No one survived such a strike. Not even her friend, the strong and confidant Marco.

She rushed to the bed, taking his hand. There was no strength, no warmth in his touch, and she leaned forward, needing to hear if he was still breathing. Wishing it were so. "Marco, please fight. I cannot lose you now. Whom do I trust if I do not have you to guide me?"

She prayed for a reply but knew none would come.

He took one final breath, and his chest did not rise again. Searing pain tore through her, wrenching out a sob. He could not be dead. She could not have lost her friend.

She felt the embrace of her sister, who, too, reached out and clasped Marco's hand.

"I'm so sorry," Alessa sobbed, laying her head upon his chest and hearing nothing but the sound of deafening silence. "I'm so terribly sorry, my friend." Knowing all the while, he never heard her apology, for he was gone.

CHAPTER 19

*T*he death of Marco left a pallor and cloak of sadness over the duke's townhouse. A week after Marco's funeral, Alessa received the invitation to the Devonshire ball, an event she had been looking forward to before the tragedy happened. Now, she could not gain an ounce of interest in the event or anything at all, if truth be told.

She was expected to attend, but to have lost a childhood friend and confidant was not something she could merely move on from. She missed Marco and was thankful to Rowan, who tried to be there to support and comfort her as much as he could when no others were about.

Thankfully the work on the women's shelter and the orphanage had kept her mind from dwelling too much over Marco. Only yesterday, they had secured the title deeds to the orphanage. The property was now secure and in her control, never under the threat of sale or eviction for those who lived there.

Alessa strode over to the window in her bedroom, looking out onto the grounds, that were extensive for

London. After dinner this evening, Aunt Rosemary wanted to go over the forthcoming invitations and discuss her movements about London the last two weeks she was to be in town.

The idea of leaving London, of leaving Rowan, made her feel even more miserable than she already did. Whatever would she do without him? How was she to continue on in Atharia, marry another when her heart belonged to someone else?

A knock sounded on her door, and she bade them enter. A shiver of awareness stole over her, and without looking, she knew Rowan was behind her.

"Your Highness, do I have permission to check your suite of rooms for any threats?"

She waved her hand, gesturing for him to start. "Of course," she said, her voice sounding tired, even to herself. And she was. Never before in her life had she ever felt so drained. Perhaps she ought to return to Atharia. Allow herself to grieve in private and away from a country forever tarnished now that it had taken her friend.

Who would be next? Her dearest Rowan? Would he be set upon and killed before her eyes too? The idea of anything happening to him made her stomach roil. She looked over her shoulder, following him about the room with her eyes. How was she ever to leave him behind? The idea left her breathless.

She swiped at her cheeks, hating her heightened emotions, but knowing she could do little about them.

"Alessa," he whispered, coming up behind her. "You are not well. I wish I could make things better for you." Her heart filled even more from his kind words.

She sniffed, turning to face him. She looked up, his shoulders blocking her view to the door. He reached out and swiped a tear from her cheek, and she leaned into his touch. "I'm sorry that you lost Marco. I can see that he meant a great deal to you."

She swallowed the lump in her throat. Her eyes stung with more unshed tears, and she knew she was losing her hold on her composure. "He was my friend, and I trusted him unconditionally." She met Rowan's eyes and lost herself a moment in his kindness.

"You can trust me, Alessa."

"Can I?" she asked, unsure why she would ask such a question, but she could not take the words back now. The man was unlike anyone she had ever had assigned to her before. Argumentative, surly, when they had first met. Danger lurked around him, and she couldn't quite shake the feeling that his life had not been an easy one.

A muscle worked at his temple before he nodded. "You can trust me. No matter what. I will not allow any harm to come to you."

She hoped that was true, for she truly did wish to live, to give to those less fortunate, marry, and have children. She may be a princess, but that did not mean she did not want everything any other woman wanted in life.

"I must return to society and attend the Devonshire ball next week. It will fall upon you to ensure safe passage to and from the townhouse and that the house itself is secure. I will have my secretary smooth away any impediments to your duties." She reached out, needing to touch him. "You will need to coordinate my security to ensure they know the plan for the evening."

"Of course. I shall ensure you're kept safe, and everyone knows their duties. I will coordinate with your secretary."

She smiled, glad to have him on her side. "You may

also need to work with my sister." She met his gaze, and something in his eyes made her shiver, made her stomach clench in a fluttery, strange kind of way.

He grinned. "I'm certain I shall tolerate the experience well enough."

Alessa could not let him leave without kissing him at least once. She reached up, taking his face in her hands and taking what she wanted. "I am certain you shall too."

*T*he Devonshire ball was everything that Alessa expected from a ball held by a duke. Everything was gold-plated, jeweled, or silk-lined, the dresses and walls alike. The home was full to the brim with guests. Many of whom had become her friends these past weeks in town.

The night was a welcome reprieve from her sadness regarding the death of Marco. That she had not suffered another attempt on her life was also promising. She could only hope that the Bow Street Runners would catch the thugs soon, and she would be well rid of them.

Alessa danced three sets with gentlemen admirers, one of them the Lord Douglas. Still, every time she stepped into the gentleman's arms, she did not feel anything other than mild friendship for the fellow.

That he had not called upon Duke Sotherton, her guardian while in London, told her in turn that perhaps his lordship no longer felt romantically inclined toward her either. Which was just as well, as she had long thought of him only as a friend.

After several wines and a glass of champagne, Alessa needed to excuse herself from the ball. She sided up to Rowan, catching his attention. "I must use the retiring room," she whispered to him.

He nodded, striding out before her and clearing a path outside the ballroom. They walked down a long corridor, multiple candelabras and a thick Aubusson rug beneath her silk slippers.

Female voices grew louder as they came to the room allocated as the retiring room for the evening. "Please wait for me here," she asked him, slipping inside. There were several ladies present and three maids willing to help the ladies who needed to freshen up.

The room quietened as the ladies slowly returned to the ball, and Alessa took a moment to have a maid address her hair at an available dressing table. The feel of the maid placing her curls back into place soothed her, and she reveled in being alone and having a moment's peace.

Splintering glass shattered across her gown, the heavy thud of something heavy hitting the floor startling her. She jumped, her maid flailing backward as a large rock tumbled not a few feet from their persons.

The door to the room slammed open, hitting the wall in its ferocity. Rowan was beside her in a second. He ran his hands over her person, checking her for any injuries before striding to the window. He looked out onto the shadowy grounds, but even Alessa could see that had there been anyone lurking in the gardens, they were either long gone or completely camouflaged by the night.

He called out to someone through the broken window, and she heard footsteps running along the pavement before the thudding of boots on the lawn met her ears.

Rowan came over to her again. Forgetting the rules of etiquette or who was about, he took her face in his hands, searching for any injuries. "Did any glass hit you? Was anything else thrown into the room?" he asked her, not letting her go.

Alessa shook her head, laying her hands upon his. "No, I am well. I think the curtains halted most of the impact from the stone." She frowned, staring at the intended weapon. "How did they know that I was in this room?"

Rowan narrowed his eyes in thought. "That is a very good point." He turned to the maid at her back. "Tell me who was in here prior to the rock being thrown. I shall need to speak with every lady present."

"I shall make a list for you, sir," the young woman stated, going over to the small desk in the room, writing out her list as promised.

"They have not declared supper yet. Do you think it safe for me to return to the ball?" She hoped she could stay merely because she was too pigheaded to leave. She did not want to be frightened home or all the way back to Atharia due to a madman's deranged beliefs that her uncle shared.

"I should think it will be safe so long as you stand on the opposite side of the room to the windows." He paused, striding to the windows in the retiring room, pulling all the heavy velvet drapes closed. "Come, we must remove you from here."

He guided her back to the ballroom, and she was pleased no one appeared aware of what had happened. She did not want anyone talking about her or who was behind these attacks. London was supposed to be fun and carefree, a time to unwind after her disastrous year in Atharia.

Anger thrummed through her that her uncle had festered such hatred for them that he would defy death itself to make her pay here in England too.

They made their way over to the opposite side of the ballroom from the windows, and she leaned into him as they stood in watch of the dancers. "When a gentleman asks me to dance, the song will place me close to the windows at times. Are you comfortable with me dancing more sets or a waltz?" she asked him, willing to trust his advice since this was what he did for a living.

"I think you have danced enough this evening, Your Highness. I cannot guarantee your safety when gliding past the bank of windows on the opposite side of the room. I hope you understand."

A footman passed, and she procured another glass of wine, wanting to numb the pain of her loss and the annoyance that she could not simply be left alone. "Then I shall imbibe to overcome my disappointment and enjoy the dancing from afar." Not that she believed his excuse entirely was due to safety concerns. She had seen Rowan's disgruntled visage when she danced with others. She was not fooled enough not to recognize jealousy when she saw it.

She smiled to herself. At least that was something she could enjoy and be happy over.

CHAPTER 20

*L*ater that evening, Rowan helped Alessa step up into the carriage. He followed her into the equipage, thumping the roof of the carriage to announce they were ready to leave—the blinds drawn, eliminating anyone seeing that Alessa was the departing guest.

They had used a side entrance that led into the Cavendish's kitchen for their escape route. No further attempts were made on Alessa, but Rowan knew they would come. The rock that had been hurled into the ladies' retiring room felt like a warning to Rowan. He knew Roberto wanted him to finish what he'd agreed to. To kill Alessa, but he would not.

Now, he would do everything in his power to keep her safe.

With the carriage making its way through Mayfair to Duke Sotherton's townhouse, Rowan shifted to sit beside Alessa, pulling her close to his side. He reached down, tipping her face up to look at him, wanting to take her mind off the troubles that surrounded them. "I did not get the opportunity this evening to tell you how beautiful you look, and so I am doing it now. You look so achingly pretty that you make my heart stop."

She grinned up at him, pleasure in her blue orbs, and he took the opportunity to kiss her. To revel in her touch and company while he could.

How was it that in only two short weeks she would sail back to Atharia, and he would never see her again?

His heart ached at the thought of it.

In a matter of time, she would marry and, soon after, become a mother. His stomach roiled at the thought of anyone other than himself having Alessa in such an intimate way. It had been bad enough this evening, watching her dance with so many eligible gentlemen—men of power and influence, of abundant wealth and titles to keep even a princess content.

He could give her nothing other than his love.

But that was not enough. She deserved so much more. So much better than what he could give.

She kissed him back with an ardor that left him breathless, left him wanting more. He hoisted her against him, taking her mouth in a searing kiss. He had wanted to touch her, hold her, comfort her these past days and could not. Her sister was always around, and the time was not right, not after the death of Marco.

Even so, he took what she offered. Had hated seeing her upset and sad. Had he been married to her, he could have comforted her, tried to keep her spirits high. Instead, he'd been forced to watch from afar as she struggled to get through each day.

"I have missed you so much, Rowan," she whispered against his lips.

He kissed her harder, reveling in her touch, the feel of

her breasts against his chest; her quickened breath and sweet little sounds of need that she made.

Their tongues entwined, hands clasped, pulled, and sought the other. He found himself rock hard, her hand over his front falls, stroking him through his breeches. They did not have long, the carriage ride from Devonshire to Duke Sotherton's was minutes only, but he was determined to take what he could. Have her in any way and as quickly as possible if that was all the time allowed them.

He pulled her onto his lap, and she gasped, moving herself closer, seeking her pleasure. She was a marvel, and he loved that she knew what she wanted. That she was willing to demand from him her needs to get what her heart desired.

He hoisted up her gown, pooling it at her waist, and reached for her. She moaned against his mouth as he stroked her wet, needy flesh. She was ready for him, and he teased her, sliding one finger into her hot core, that contracted about his digit.

"Rowan," she gasped, ripping at his front falls. "I need you. Now," she demanded.

He did not stop her. He wanted her just as much. His cock sprang free of his breeches into her hand, and he sucked in a breath as she stroked him harder still.

"I want you too. Take your pleasure, Princess," he commanded her.

A wicked light entered her eyes, and she came over him farther, lowering herself onto his dick with achingly, tormenting slowness.

He clasped her hips, helping her fall into a delicious rhythm. Alessa did not take long to learn the ways of love-making in a carriage. She rode him fast, her tight cunny milking him to a fevered pitch. He breathed deep, wanting her to shatter in his arms, to take what she wanted before he found his release.

Rowan thrust into her, taking her lips, suckling her tongue as she fucked him. He was mad for her, adored her.

Loved her?

He held her harder, wanting to please her in all ways. She mewled against his mouth, and he knew she was close. "Oh, Rowan," she panted, kissing him and leaving his mind to whirl.

She shattered in his arms, riding him with a furor that he was unable to deny. He came hard, pumping his seed into her womb, a small part of him hoping it would take root.

He wanted the woman in his arms. Not just tonight or the last two weeks of the Season, but always. The carriage turned, and a part of his conscience warned that they were not far from the mews.

A lopsided smile lifted her lips, her eyes hazy with satisfaction and the remnants of pleasure.

"We need to move, my darling. We are almost back at your home."

She ran her hand over his jaw before kissing him slowly, her tongue tangling with his, and in no rush to move. He threw himself into her touch, uncertain when he would have her again in his arms.

"I cannot give you up, Rowan. Please do not make me," she asked of him, sadness clouding her blue orbs.

He sighed, wishing he did not have to let her go either but not seeing any way forward to allow such a union. It was simply impossible. Rowan lifted her and helped her adjust her gown on the squabs. Her hair was as perfect as when she'd stepped up into the carriage, and other than the slightly rosier cheeks, she did not look like a woman thoroughly fucked in the back of a carriage.

"We will discuss it tomorrow. Now we must depart," he said, moving to sit on the opposite seat, watching her and wanting her again in equal measure.

She looked as displeased as he felt.

"I hate that I cannot touch you, that I cannot be with you whenever I want. I no longer wish to live in this way. Tell me you feel the same, Rowan."

He frowned, knowing he should lie to her. Tell her that he did not feel the same. That there was no hope for them. But he could not. "I know," he sighed, running a hand through his hair. "I hate being away from you too. But there is nothing to be done for it. We are from opposite worlds, Alessa. There is no changing who I am."

She glared at him, her lips thinning into a displeased line. "I do not care about any of that. I know what I want, and that is you. It does not matter to me where you're from or who your family is. I will welcome them all if you let me."

He sighed, wishing that were the case. "I have no family, Alessa. I have not had anyone since I was a young boy. I do not even know my age."

Her mouth opened and closed several times, a confusing line to her brow, before she said, "How can you not know your age?" she asked him.

He shrugged, having asked himself that question many times. "I have lived on my own since I was a small boy. I do not remember my parents or siblings if I had any. I only remember I was as young as a six or seven year old. My life was hard and dangerous, and I learned to survive more so than worry about how old I was."

She reached out, taking his hand. "I'm so very sorry, Rowan. Was your life so very bad?" she asked him.

He cringed, the memory of his life never an easy one. "I worked as a chimney sweep for some months. The man who hired me was kind and fed me dinner, but he died, and I was soon on my own again. I remember being taken to several orphanages, but none were as loving and clean and warm as the one you will be helping in Seven Dials."

She bit her bottom lip, listening to his every word. A flood of memories, none of them good, burst free, and he found himself unable to tell her all that happened to him as a child. "One orphanage was worse than the others. The priests there were...well," he said, swallowing the bile that rose in his throat. "They were cruel to the boys especially, and I was one of those boys. I ran away, unable to bear another second in that den of evil, and I've lived on the street ever since.

"I fought, starved, stole, and killed to survive. That is not who a princess marries, not in the real world and not even in a make-believe one. Some of us are destined for greatness, and others, myself included, are not. That is the way of the world, cruel as that world is when something as sweet and pure, kind and gentle as yourself crosses the path of a man like me and makes me want what I cannot have."

She moved over to sit beside him, her arms wrapping about him, holding him close. "I will kill those who harmed you." He felt her shudder in his arms, and he knew she was crying. Rowan wrapped his arms about her, rubbing her back in comfort.

"Do not cry, my darling. There is nothing to be done about it now. it was a long time ago."

"I wish I could take all your pain away," she said, leaning back and meeting his eyes.

He wished she could too. "You do take the sting out of my life just by being near me. You are the first woman to see past my outer shell, and I shall always hold you dear in my heart for giving no judgment on my character and past." The small part she knew of, at least.

"I would never judge you. You mean everything to me. You have saved me and kept me safe. How can I not love you, Rowan?"

He stilled, his heart thumping loudly in his ears. "You cannot love me, Alessa. I'll not allow that. That is too much."

"It is not enough," she said, pulling him back to look at her when he steadfastly refused to meet her eyes. He did not want to fall into her blue orbs, for to fall into her soul was to fall hard and forever.

"I want you in my life, Rowan. Now and forever. I do not care what my sister thinks, what anyone does. I want you. I love you, and you must marry me, or I'll be forever heartbroken."

His heart stopped at her words. She could not marry him. He could not marry her. There was too much between them. The divide was too great. He had met her only because he was to kill her. She would never forgive such a sin should she know the truth. And yet, he wanted to curse everyone to the devil who told him he could not have her. That he could not love her as she loved him.

"I would marry you tomorrow. You must know that. But you need to understand what marriage to me would mean for you. You will be ostracized by society. No one would want a princess who married her guard as one of their acquaintances. A penniless street urchin without family or name. I have nothing to give you, and you deserve the world."

She clasped his shoulders, shaking him a little. "Do you love me, Rowan? Really love me," she insisted. "As much as I love you?"

He read the hope and fear in her eyes, and he knew he could not lie. "I love and adore you so much that at times I'm crazed with want and fear of you."

A slow smile spread across her face, and she wrapped her arms around his neck, kissing him. "That is very good news then, for that is all that matters. You will see." She nodded, a determined note to her words. "I will get my way, and you will be my husband. I will not accept anything less, and nor will I go through life regretting my choice. I want you, not some other nameless prince. Just you."

The carriage rocked to a halt and dipped as the two guards on the back of the carriage jumped down. Alessa threw him a satisfied grin just as the door opened and a guard helped her down.

Rowan followed behind, forcing his pulse to calm and his hope to subside. There was little point in dreaming for a miracle. His life had never gone the way he had hoped, and he had little doubt that in regards to Alessa, it would be no different.

He would lose her in the end. He was to have been her killer, and nothing and no one could go back and change his previous decision, to murder her for blunt. When she found out the truth, she would leave him just like everyone else in his life to date. And deservedly so. He was not for her. That was just the way of the world for hapless nobodies like him.

CHAPTER 21

*A*lessa all but floated into her room after leaving Rowan and skidded to a stop at the sight of her sister. Holly stood at the window, looking out onto the gardens at the back of the townhouse.

"Holly, are you well?" Alessa curtsied, slipping off her shawl and laying it over one of the settees before the fire. Her sister turned, clasping her hands at her front, and Alessa could see that she was not well. That there was something very wrong. Her stomach churned, and she steeled herself to listen to whatever it was that was troubling Holly.

"I think you ought to sit, Alessa, for what I'm about to tell you is, I fear, going to hurt you very much."

Holly's tone brooked no argument, and she did as she bade, lowering herself on one of the chairs. "What is it?" she asked, taking a calming breath. Was Elana safe and well? Had something happened to Drew? What?!

Holly joined her. She studied Alessa a moment before rallying herself to speak. "I have received news this evening from the Bow Street Runners, and it is disturbing information."

Alessa frowned, growing ever impatient to hear what it was. "And, what have you found out?"

"Several things," Holly continued. "The first thing you ought to know is that our uncle is indeed dead, but his closest confidant, Roberto Delenzo is behind the attacks on your person. He has gone to ground, but two of his henchmen have been apprehended and are spending their first night in Newgate."

Alessa gasped, remembering Roberto, a man who was like a shadow to her uncle—following him about Atharia and doing his nasty bidding. It made sense that the fool would continue what her uncle had started here in England. "That is good news, is it not?" she stated, relieved to hear that at least they knew who their foe was, and they could go after him with more vigor.

Holly shook her head, pain crossing her features. "There is more. Upon the arrest of the two men who worked for Roberto, they were persuaded to name anyone else who worked to strike out at you." Holly left her chair and kneeled before Alessa's, taking her hands. "Darling, they named Rowan, Mr. Oakley as the man who Roberto hired to infiltrate our security, gain access to you and form a close bond to strike when the timing was right. He was hired to kill you, sweetheart. I'm so sorry," Holly stated, not letting go of her.

Alessa wrenched free, standing. The room spun, and she clasped the mantel to anchor herself. Rowan? No, it could not be. He loved her. He had stated that fact only minutes before she entered the house. He would not agree to do such an underhanded, unhonorable thing to her or anyone. "You are mistaken. That is not true," she stated, shaking her head. Bile rose in her throat, and she ran to the chamber pot, vomiting up the contents of her stomach.

She heard her sister pour water somewhere in the room before coming over to her and passing her the glass. "Here, sister, drink this. It will settle your stomach. I know this will be a great shock to you, but you must believe me. What I say is true. I would never lie to you. You know that."

Alessa could not believe it at all. She took the glass of water and had a sip, putting it aside just as quickly. She stood, pacing the floor, her gown swishing in her wake. "Rowan would not do such a thing. He's an honorable man. A kind man," she argued, thinking of all the wonderful moments they had together. All the times he'd held her in his arms, kissed and touched her, made love to her, brought her so much pleasure.

No, her mind inwardly screamed. Holly was wrong. She had to be. To think of Rowan, a cold-blooded murderer, a liar, a man who had only stated such things to her to turn about and kill her, could not be right.

"If he was hired to kill me, then why has he not? He has had plenty of opportunities, believe me," she admitted, knowing the time to lie, to deny how she felt for him and what she had done was long over. "I have given myself to him, Holly."

Her sister gasped, her eyes going wide with alarm. "Tell me you did not, Alessa," she chided, coming over to her and clasping her shoulders. "Tell me you did not sleep with him. He's a murderer, a hired killer, and one who has you in his sights. Tell me you did not allow him to fool you so easily."

Alessa swallowed the lump in her throat, the panic that continued to build within her. Her hands shook, and her legs felt feeble. "I love him. I have fallen in love with him. How could I not be with him in all ways?"

Holly let her go, her sister's face ashen with alarm. "He is bad, Alessa. To his very core, he is rotten. No man of honor, no man who loved another, agreed to kill the very person they supposedly adore. You have been fooled, sister. But thankfully, we have discovered this nasty plot before anything happened to you."

"He could have killed me weeks ago. We have been alone multiple times. I do not believe that Roberto Delenzo and his thugs are telling the truth. They are the liars. Rowan has done nothing but keep me from harm, never placing me before it."

Holly shook her head, disregarding her words. "We leave tonight on a ship back to Atharia. Rowan is right now downstairs in the custody of the Bow Street Runners, and he will face the full force of the English law. He will hang by morning. I will not leave England until I'm assured of it," Holly declared, determination in her tone.

Alessa could not believe it. Not until she heard it from Rowan, which of course he would refute all these claims, and all would be well. He would make Holly see that Roberto and his thugs were liars. That they were the criminals, and they had hit out at Rowan to hurt her. That was their plan.

"I need to speak to him."

"Absolutely not," Holly returned, glaring at her, no longer her sister but her powerful, demanding queen.

"I need to speak to him, Holly. I need to hear it from him, or I shall never believe you." Which, of course, she did not. None of these lies were true.

Her sister paced, mumbling under her breath. Alessa could not make out what she said, but she could guess well enough. Her sister was torn, enraged, and most definitely betrayed. But all would be well. Rowan would make this right. He would put a stop to this nonsense and make Holly see that he may have had a hard life, but that did not make him a killer for hire.

"I cannot allow it. He could finish what he came here to do in the first place. It is too risky."

Alessa crossed her arms. "No, if you want me to leave London by morning, I need to hear what you accuse Rowan of from him. If I do not, I shall never believe you, nor will I ever forgive you if you take me from the man I love, and he is innocent of the crime you lay at his door."

Holly narrowed her eyes, her mouth pinched. "I will ensure he is tied up further before you speak to him. I will not allow it under any other circumstances. If you're in agreement, then I shall let you speak with him before we go." Holly moved to the door, opening it before waiting out in the passage for Alessa.

With one final deep breath, Alessa followed her, determined to find out the truth and put a stop to all this madness, for to believe the alternative would surely make her mad if Holly turned out to be telling her the truth.

His treachery could not be so. It was simply unfathomable.

*R*owan sat in the library, tied with immovable rope around his chest, arms, wrists, and ankles. There was not the slightest chance he was escaping these bonds, and he could only imagine what was going through Alessa's mind right at this moment.

Her sister would have no doubt notified her of his capture. Not his finest moment, but it was the least he deserved. He was the murderer they accused him of being. Worse still, he was working here for one reason and one reason only—to kill Alessa.

He ground his teeth, self-loathing riding him hard. The door to the library opened, and he caught the sweet scent of jasmine and orange and knew Alessa was behind him.

"They allowed you to see me. I did not think your sister would relent," he stated. The queen had been adamant she would see him hang. That she had never trusted him, and her gut reaction to his presence in the house was right all along.

Rowan had denied the charges, of course, but there was truth to what she said. He was a killer. Granted, he only killed degenerative men who deserved to meet their maker, but that did not change who he was and what he was doing here.

Alessa came about the chair, facing him. She still wore the gown she had worn to the Devonshire ball. The very one he had lifted and taken his fill of her only an hour before.

How had it been that his life had changed so much in such a short period? The night had been young, and he had intended to travel down to Aldgate to take care of the last two men who worked to kill Alessa but had not made it to Piccadilly Road before the Queen of Atharia's men had clubbed him from behind and bundled him up in ropes.

His head throbbed, and he could taste blood in his mouth. No doubt on his fall to the ground, his face had taken the brunt.

She gasped, her face paling, and he guessed that his injuries were worse than first thought.

"Ask me, Alessa," he stated, seeing no point in delaying

the inevitable. They had never stood a chance, now perhaps she would agree with him for a change.

The sadness that entered her trusting blue orbs broke his heart, and he cursed himself to hell for hurting her so. Should he have his time again, he would never have accepted such a mission to harm her. That he had in the first place made his stomach churn.

"Is it true, Rowan?" she asked him, watching his every move. "Were you hired to kill me?"

He nodded once, watching as his life slipped from his fingers. The woman he loved grow ever distant from him. For there was no keeping her after this. No redemption for his corrupt self. "It is true. Roberto Delenzo hired me to kill you for reasons only he could understand. I was to be paid a handsome sum, and that is all of my dealings with the man to date."

Her mouth opened and closed several times, but no words spilled forth. He could see she was struggling with the news, that his words broke her as much as they hurt him.

"When did you plan on killing me? Was it tonight? The first time we met? When?" she asked, her voice unnervingly calm.

He wished he could go to her, wrap her in his arms, fall to his knees and beg for forgiveness. He tested the ropes bound around him and found the action only tightened their hold. "Whenever the opportunity arose, which I will admit occurred often. But upon meeting you and getting to know you these past weeks, I saw that you were a good person with a genuine heart. I could not kill you. Instead, I fell in love with you, and I knew that the only people I would kill were those who wished you harm."

Her swallow was almost audible. She slumped against

the desk, her knuckles white from holding the mahogany wood so tight. "Are you saying you killed Roberto's men?"

"Of course I did. You were there when I killed Piedro and Dino, if you remember. They were hired by your uncle's man and would have harmed you had I not been at the tavern. I would not allow that. I could not allow anything to happen to you, then or now."

She thought over his words a moment before she said, "The last two men other than yourself are locked away in Newgate, but Roberto has gone to ground. The Runners are looking for him now, but I do not hold out much hope. He will disappear, and no doubt slink back to cause more mischief another day."

The thought that Alessa would always be in harm's way made his blood pump cold. How would he survive wherever he ended up next with the thought that Alessa could be injured or killed? He would rather die than live a life constantly wondering about her. He would be a shell of a man who did not live at all with such a future.

Not that you have one, his mind reminded him.

"Have me freed, and I will kill him, Alessa. I promise you, on my honor, that he will not survive the night."

She scoffed, laughing, the sound brittle and cold. "You? Upon your honor? Well, that is something new, I suppose. An honorable killer, no matter if you only kill those who deserve it. Like any of your other victims, what if they too had been put about as bad, evil people and were not. I am not wicked, and yet you thought to snap my neck, did you not? Or were you going to use a knife or gun? Tell me, how would you have killed me?" she demanded of him.

Rowan had never thought to delve further into the men he had killed in the past for their crimes, taking the victim's words as truth. Mayhap that was wrong. By God, had he not come to know Alessa, she would already be gone. He closed his eyes, thankful he had not acted as swiftly as he normally would.

"The Hamilton ball was where I was going to kill you. I followed you into the darkened passage, and no one knew where we were. The opportunity arose, and I even reached up and clasped your face, ready to break your pretty neck, if you remember. But you looked at me with such longing, such hope that I froze. I knew at that moment that you were different and that I had made a grave mistake. One that I have been trying to correct since."

Alessa looked at him as if she did not know who he was. He wanted to scream that she did know, that she was the only person who knew him at all. Never had he ever opened up to anyone as much as he opened up to her. He loved and adored her. He could not lose her now, but he no longer held that choice. The truth was out, and with it, so too did it bring an end to their love.

She would hate him now.

"How could you?" She strode up to him, lifting his chin, her fingers hard against his flesh, pinching him a little. "What a fool I have been. Here I thought that you were the first man who wanted to kiss me enough that you would risk my reputation and your life to do so. And all the while, you wanted to snap my neck like a twig. You stood before me, a stranger whom I trusted and should not have trusted at all. You're a bastard," she snapped, pushing him away and striding to stand around the opposite side of the desk.

"I am a bastard," he agreed. "God knows it is unlikely my parents were married, but I do love you, Alessa. I will never love anyone as much as I love you. I'm sorry I took the job from Delenzo. I was desperate. I have nothing. I've never had anything. All my life, I've struggled, and I could not see my way out. The payment would secure me for life, and I could not turn it away. But I promise you, your life was never in danger from me. Not really.

"The moment I saw you, as hard as I was upon you when we first met, it was because I knew I had made a mistake. That there was no chance that I could hurt one hair on your precious head. I knew that my only mission was keeping you alive, and if you let me go, that is what I shall do. Delenzo will be nothing more than a bad memory, and so too will I. I will not seek you out or contact you again. I will disappear and allow you to move on with your life, marry another and be happy. That is all that I want for you. I know there is no chance for us anymore."

She swiped at her cheeks, her eyes sparkling with tears. He cursed, hating that he'd hurt her so. Damn it all to hell. He hated himself right at that moment.

"Very well," she said, coming around the desk and swiping up a small knife he had not seen sitting on the surface of the desk. She cut the ropes about his feet and hands and then his chest, giving him his freedom.

She stood back, keeping the knife in her hand. "There is a hidden servants' door to the right of the bookshelf over there," she said, pointing to that part of the room. "Follow it to the very end, and it will bring you out to a hatch in the duke's mews. It was shown to me upon arriving here as a way of escape should anything happen to me or my life was threatened inside the house." She laughed, but the sound was hollow. "How stupid of us all not to know that the threat was in the house all along. That I allowed that threat to enter my bed."

Rowan felt the blow of her words like a physical punch to his gut. He did not try to beg for her to forgive him, to give him one last memory of her sweet lips. Instead, he strode to the servants' door and pushed it open, seeing the darkened corridor beyond. Swiping up a candle, he cast one last look at Alessa, imprinting her on his mind, his memory, and left.

He would not see her again, and his heart stopped at the realization of it.

CHAPTER 22

*R*owan knew that Delenzo would try one last time to strike at Alessa, even if it were from his own hand. He sat in wait in an old abandoned warehouse that overlooked the Port of London. London Bridge just off to the side of where the ships docked. Here he could see several vessels of differing sizes docked, one of which was bigger and grander than the others, but without a flag.

The ship would have to be the Royal Family of Atharia's and the one that would take Alessa hundreds of miles across the sea from him.

He deserved what he got. Hell, he deserved far more than a broken heart. That Alessa had let him go, had not allowed her sister or the London Runners to mete out their punishment was more than he deserved. He ought to hang for the crimes he'd dealt out to others. People, now he could not help but wonder who were as innocent as Alessa had been.

He cringed, hoping that was not the case.

A shadowy movement near a stacked group of wooden

crates caught his eye, and he watched, wondering if Delenzo had finally made his appearance.

He would not allow anything to happen to Alessa or her sister. They would depart on the ship, safe and whole, and no bastard madman would halt their journey.

The docks were quiet and still at this hour of the night, well past midnight, although some candles were burning in windows and ship hulls. A watchman paced the deck of the royal ship, a saber in his hand, but from his relaxed stance, he had not seen the assailant lurking near the crates.

It did not matter, for Rowan had seen him, and he would not succeed in his mission, no matter what it was. If Rowan could do one honorable thing for Alessa before he watched her sail away, it was this. Remove the last vestiges, the last of their troubles in Atharia and here in England once and for all.

*A*lessa pulled the dark cloak about her farther as she sat in the carriage, listening to the wheels roll over cobbles and wood as they made their way out onto the London docks.

The scent of sea air caught her attention and, with it, the realization that soon they would be on their way home. Hundreds of miles from Rowan. Where would he go after what had happened here? She doubted he would stay in England. He had mentioned the Americas. Would he travel there? Would he marry another?

She clutched at her stomach, swallowing the bile that rose in her throat at the thought of such a thing. The muffled talk of her sister to her husband caught her attention, and she looked over at Holly and Drew. They were as close and loving as the day they married.

She had hoped that she, too, had found such a love. Disappointment stabbed at her that she had not. Her love affair with Rowan had been a lie. A plan concocted by him to merely get near her person to kill her. She shivered, still unable to comprehend such a heinous act.

How could he have made such sweet love to her, declared his feelings, and have been working for Delenzo the entire time? She had been fooled, but never again. Never again would she ever allow a man to get close to her, to trick her in such a way.

She would never marry now.

The carriage rocked to a halt before the door opened, and one of their trusted guards helped her step down. Alessa followed Holly and Drew, all of them flanked by multiple guards as they made their way to the ship.

A commotion to her left made her glance that way, and she caught the sight of a bloodied knife finding its purpose in one of their guard's necks.

What happened next was a blur. Shots fired into the quiet night, men dropped as the bullets met their mark, and then she saw him. Roberto Delenzo stood not a few feet from her, his crazed, bloodshot eyes pinning her to the spot.

She heard her sister scream for her to run, and she glanced over her shoulder to find Holly and Drew being hoisted toward the ship. But she was not. She stood, flanked by two guards, but Delenzo stood before her, breathing deep with his maddening, unhinged hatred of her.

"Now, I shall get at your sister where it will most hurt

her. By killing you, Princess, she will know she has failed as queen. That she failed you."

A cold chill stole down Alessa's spine, and she moved back, allowing her guards to stand before her.

Delenzo laughed, the sound crazed before her guards clasped her arms, hoisting her toward him. She screamed, kicking out at them as best she could in her traveling gown and cloak. "What are you doing?" she demanded, her voice high-pitched with panic.

In the distance, she heard Holly shout orders, her sister's voice as panicked as hers.

She stole a look at the two guards in cohorts with Delenzo, noting their glee. Was everyone working for her dead uncle? This could not be true. "You will not win, Delenzo. Kill me here, and you will die here too. I can promise you that."

He shrugged, walking up to her, the large, bowed knife coming to rest on her throat. She stilled, feeling the sting as the mere touch of the knife cut her flesh. "What is life anyway, but days and nights of nothing in particular. You and your family do not deserve your privilege. I will take yours and make your sister suffer until the day she dies. That will be satisfying enough for me."

"You're mad," she spat, glaring. If she were to die, she would not go down simmering and swooning like a delicate flower. That was not who she was, nor ever had been.

Footsteps on wooden planks sounded behind her, and Delenzo's attention snapped toward the ship. "Move another inch, and her head comes off. Do you understand?"

The footsteps stopped, and Alessa wondered if he would really act so barbaric. Was she going to be killed in such a way? She had always hoped her death would occur in her sleep, late in her life when she had children and grandchildren surrounding her.

Not here on the cold, London docks with the stench of rotting garbage and fish guts stinging her nose.

Delenzo smirked. "Now, where was I?" he asked, meeting her gaze.

"She was supposed to be my kill," a familiar voice sounded from a nearby warehouse before the sight of Rowan came into view. He strode toward them without a care, and her heart stopped in her chest.

He did not mean what he said. He could not.

Had she made a terrible mistake in letting him go? Had she allowed a liar, a killer a second chance at earning his blunt from her death? She sent up a silent prayer that she had not. She could stand most things, but to think she was fooled a second time by the man she loved, she could not face, not even mere minutes before death.

"Come, Rowan, you may still do the honors." Delenzo chuckled, gesturing for Rowan to join him faster.

Alessa felt herself losing her composure. Rowan would not hurt her. He would not. No matter what had come to pass between them, he would not deceive her in that.

She prayed she was right.

Rowan joined them, taking the knife from Delenzo and twisting and turning it before her face. "What would you like me to do to her?" He chuckled. "Well, what else would you like me to do to her? I've already tupped the wench. She wasn't bad either," he quipped.

The guards holding her chuckled, one being so bold as to lean against her and smell her hair.

"Guv, can we not have her too? Before she's run in?"

Alessa hoped to see some reaction on Rowan's visage,

but he did not even flinch at their disgusting words. Merely watched her with cold indifference.

She kicked out, landing a solid blow to Delenzo's chest. He stumbled and righted himself quickly enough. "Bastards," she yelled. "I'll hate you forever if you mean what you say," she said to Rowan.

A muscle worked in his jaw before a blow, startling in its velocity, landed across her cheek. She gasped, having not expected Delenzo to do such a thing. Why, however, she wasn't certain. He was a killer, just as all these men who held her were.

"I have no issue with her being taken," Delenzo said, meeting Rowan's gaze. "Do you want another turn before we gut the bitch?"

She gasped, her vision blurring. She wasn't sure if it was from the blow to her face or the tears that now streamed down her cheeks. She could hear her sister command the guards, but the moment Holly did, the knife was at her neck again, this time at the hand of Rowan.

She met his gaze, begging him to stop, to not hurt her. "Rowan, please do not do this." She would say anything right at this moment if only it concluded this nightmare.

"Close your eyes, Alessa," Rowan commanded, his tone different from before, calm and with an edge of determination. She did as he bade. This was it, her life. Her heart crumbled in her chest, and she sagged in the arms of the men holding her. What did it matter anymore? Life itself had no meaning. Not now that Rowan had betrayed her a second time, and the last.

· · ·

169

*R*owan steeled himself and took a calming breath as he watched Alessa close her eyes. The moment she did, he made his move. With a flick of his wrist, the blade he held to Alessa's neck shot out and sliced across the guard to the right's throat. Blood splattered, and his hold on Alessa ceased. He wrenched her from the other man's hold, using his moment of shock to place himself between them. He pulled out the gun hidden in his trews and shot the bastard between the eyes.

The man fell, shock upon his features. Rowan then turned to Delenzo, a man far savvier and battle-weary than anyone present, himself included. He reached back, ensuring Alessa was behind him, safe and away from the bastard.

Her hand reached out, taking his, and his heart stuttered to a stop in his chest, knowing she was well, so far had been reasonably unharmed.

"I should have known that your delay in killing the princess meant that you had succumbed to her will—you weak bastard. You could have had more money than you knew what to do with, and yet you save her. Allow her to live her life of luxury while you rot away in the East End, fighting for every coin you can get your hands on."

"Better that than be a traitor like you. I have not only fallen under her spell. I love her, and you will have to kill me if you want to touch a hair on her head."

"That is done easily enough," Delenzo said, moving to strike him as quick as the snake that he was. And the dance for life and death began.

CHAPTER 23

With horror, Alessa watched as Rowan fought Delenzo. The fight she knew would be to the death, but who would win? The sound of flesh hitting flesh, the sight of the blood, the thumping and snapping of blows made her cringe.

The guards who had stood back rushed toward her. One threw her over his shoulder, and she realized that Drew was running with her in his arms toward the ship. Not a guard at all, but her brother-in-law.

She punched his back, wanting to stay with Rowan to ensure he survived. What if he needed her help? What if Delenzo killed him, and she was not there for him in his final moments, just as he was there for her.

"Put me down! Drew, please, put me down," she begged.

"Do not under any circumstances put my sister down, husband," she heard Holly command, and Alessa knew her fight was moot. Drew would never go against his wife and queen, not for anything and especially not to put Alessa's life at risk yet again.

She was dumped on the deck of the boat, and she ran to the handrail, looking back on the docks as the fight between Rowan and Delenzo escalated. "Go and help him," she screamed when Delenzo held Rowan down on the ground, laying punch after punch against his face.

Oh God, he was going to die. "Holly, please, if you do one thing for me, please help Rowan. He saved me. He was loyal to me at the time that I thought I would die. Please, do not let me let him down too."

Holly looked back onto the dock. The gangplank pulled onto the deck of the ship and all their men aboard. She turned to one of the guards who held a musket. He ran over to her, bowing.

"Your Majesty?" he asked, waiting for commands.

"Shoot Delenzo when you have a safe shot at doing so. We will be rid of him once and for all," her sister mumbled under her breath as she turned away from the sight of the two men.

Alessa would thank her later, but she frowned, fear curdling her blood at the darkness of the docks. There was little light. What if their marksman hit Rowan instead of Delenzo?

No, that would not happen. He would not miss. Alessa walked up to the man preparing his shot on the deck of the boat. "Do not miss," she cautioned. "Delenzo only, do you understand?" she affirmed.

The marksman nodded, leaning over his weapon, his eyes narrowing as he took in the target.

Alessa held her breath, watching, praying. The blade of the knife that was held at her neck was lifted by Delenzo.

Oh dear God, Rowan was going to be stabbed.

Just as she was about to scream, a shot rang out,

making her start. Delenzo slumped over Rowan before being pushed to the side, and Rowan scuttled out from beneath him.

She sighed, relief pouring through her. He was well. He had survived.

The ship started to move down the Thames, the sails flapping as they caught a breeze, taking them out to sea and back to her home.

Alessa stood on the deck watching Rowan. He walked to the edge of the docks, watching the ship move farther away. She mouthed thank you, the sight of her life, her heart growing ever smaller in the night before the swirl of fog took his form and swallowed it up as if he had never been.

But he had been. Rowan, the love of her life, her soul mate and savior, had been real, and she loved him dearly. She and her family owed him her life, and she would be forever grateful.

Even if she never saw him again, she forgave him his sins and prayed that he found peace. "I love you," she declared to the inky blackness of the Thames, knowing there would be no reply.

There was not.

CHAPTER 24

Two years later

*A*lessa stood beside her sister and queen as their sister, Elena, dipped into a regal curtsy before the crown, and was officially out in society in Atharia. Holly stood, kissing Elena's cheeks before Elena curtsied again and moved back out of the room, as was expected of her.

The line of debutantes was a yearly ball that Holly enjoyed growing up and had wanted to resurrect after their uncle's coup attempt halted them for two years. But this year, they had made a choice to resurrect them, and she was pleased for Elena and the other debutantes that they had.

"There are so many foreigners here this evening. Did you see Lord Douglas is here and with his new countess? She's very beautiful," Holly commented, flicking her chin in his lordship's direction.

Alessa glanced out over the sea of heads as the debutante progression ended, and the room became the ballroom for the night's entertainment.

Footmen carried around trays of drinks and food, the house of Atharia preferring to serve small dishes of delicacies to their guests rather than stopping to serve supper as the English had done.

"I'm happy for his lordship. Lord Douglas deserves to be fortunate." And he did. Everyone did, in fact. Her opinion on love had not changed, even though she had not been so successful herself.

To think that it had been two years since she had seen Rowan still left a hollow void inside her chest that Alessa never thought would fill. Even though her sister had two children now who kept Alessa busy being the best aunt she could, it did not make the loss of Rowan any easier to bear.

He had saved her. Had been there for her when she needed him most. Had redeemed himself when she had thought him irredeemable.

Alessa rallied herself to push the thought of him aside. He was gone. He probably lived in the Americas now. Far away from Atharia and the woman he once loved.

Holly clasped her hand, squeezing it a little. "I wish you nothing but to be happy again, Alessa. I hope you will be," she said, throwing her a wistful smile.

Alessa frowned, wondering why her sister would say such a thing. Had her longing for Rowan been obvious to everyone at court? It was a possibility. She often caught herself lost in the memories of her time in England.

A tall gentleman bowed before her, and she turned, ready to accept another dance that would lead nowhere except back to her position beside her sister until another gentleman asked her yet again.

"Waltz with me, Princess?"

The familiar, gravely baritone brought her up short.

She gasped, waiting with bated breath as he stood straight, meeting her eyes. Her mind whirled, the room spun, and Holly chuckled at her side.

"Rowan?" she asked, unsure it was him. It looked like Rowan, tall and broad-shouldered, chiseled jaw and striking eyes that she wanted to drown in, and yet it did not look like him.

The man before her was dressed in evening attire, silk breeches, and polished knee-high boots. His superfine coat fit him like a second skin, the silver waistcoat and cravat complementing his attire. She had never seen him so well-dressed. He looked like a lord.

"How is it that you're here?" she asked him, her mind unable to comprehend his presence.

"I had him brought to Atharia, Alessa dear," Holly stated, matter-of-fact. "Two years and you were still not happy, and I knew I had to do something about it."

Alessa turned to her sister. "Rowan isn't a gentleman. You told me I could not marry him."

Holly's lips twisted into a wry smile. "I knighted him upon his arrival yesterday for his bravery and duty toward the crown and you, a princess of Atharia." Holly leaned toward her. "You can marry him now, sister. He is Sir Oakley, perfectly acceptable for a princess."

"Shall we?" Rowan asked again, holding out his arm for her and throwing her a wicked grin.

Like a dream, she placed her hand on his arm, allowing him to lead her out onto the floor. She could not look away from him. He was warm. The same scent of citrus wafted from his skin, reminding and confirming it really was Rowan at her side.

He swung her into the dance, merging into the waltz and other couples seamlessly. "I did not think I would see you again," he stated, his hand warm on her back, his thumb stroking her skin and leaving her breathless.

Alessa shivered. "Thank you for saving me, Rowan. I owe you my life and so much more than that. I wish I had been able to tell you in England. To see you and not be able to thank you for that day, well, it broke my heart."

He shook his head, dismissing her words. "You owe me nothing. It is I who begs for forgiveness. I hate that I ever agreed to do what Delenzo wanted. I shall never forgive myself for putting you in danger, of betraying your trust as I did. I do not deserve your forgiveness or love."

Oh, but he did. And no matter the time that had passed, she loved him still. "Unfortunately, you do not get to decide what I feel or want," she declared yet again to him. "Seeing you again, touching you," she said, running her hands up his arms to wrap about his neck, "it is like a dream come true. I have missed you so very much."

Rowan wrapped his arms about her, pulling her near. Their closeness still wasn't enough. She wanted more. "Tell me what you have been doing these past two years. I imagined you on distant shores in the Americas, happy in your new life. A woman and children at your side." Not that she had liked that imagining, but then, so long as he was happy, so too would she have been for him.

"No," he declared with a little bit of revulsion. "If you remember, your sister returned to London last Season. I heard she was in town, and as shameful as it was, I waited on the docks as the ship arrived. I was so hopeful that you would be with her and so disappointed when you were not. I asked for an audience with her, and surprisingly she agreed."

Alessa had not heard a word of this. "Holly never said a word about it."

He grinned. "I asked her not to. I offered my apologies to your sister."

"And did she grant you forgiveness?" Alessa asked, knowing she had because Rowan was here, in her arms and hers forever.

"No, she threw me in Newgate for three days."

"What?" Alessa gasped, her heart stopping at the thought of such imprisonment. "Holly threw you in jail?"

Rowan chuckled. "For three days, but I did think that I was there for the duration of my life. Until I was released and your sister was in the carriage that took me back to my rooms in Spitalsfield."

Alessa could not believe any of this. She had no idea any of this occurred. She would have a strongly worded talk with Holly when she was ready to let Rowan out of her sight. "What happened then?" she asked, intrigued.

"She put me to work on your women's shelter. I've learned the trade of a builder and have helped bring to fruition your dream of the sanctuary for women. I also work as a guard and support to the children's orphanage. It enabled me to remain close to you, even when the distance between us was so great."

Somewhere between their words, they had stopped dancing and were standing in the middle of the ballroom floor. She did not care who heard or watched them. Nothing mattered. All that did was Rowan, and he was before her, in her arms, and she would never let him go again.

"You helped complete my two projects?" She blinked, fighting back the tears. How wonderful he was. He did not have to be so. His upbringing, his hard years as a child, and his youth could have hardened the man before her. Made him loathe people and become part of the problem instead of the solution. But instead, he had seen a better way. He may have tripped a time or two on his journey to the life that he wanted, but he had finally arrived at the destination that was his to claim.

A future with her.

"It is like a dream for me seeing you too," he admitted, leaning his forehead against hers. "I love you still, Alessa. Tell me that you will be mine. Now and forever. Be my wife," he asked her, kissing her quickly. "Marry me, my darling princess."

Alessa sniffed, her mind a kaleidoscope of nerves and excitement, of hope and dreams. She nodded, knowing that, in this case, she did not have a choice. The heart wanted what it wanted, and hers beat only for the man in her arms.

"I will marry you, my darling love."

Rowan smiled, his eyes alight with pleasure. He took her lips in a searing kiss that made her toes curl in her silk slippers. Alessa forgot where they were and who was about them and kissed him back. She leaned up on tiptoe and took her fill of him, kissed him with all the love and adoration she could muster. And after two years of living without her heart, she had a lot to give to Rowan.

The sound of clapping, of laughter, oohs, and ahhs sounded about them, and she ignored them all. Instead, the kiss went on, needy and with tears shed by both of them.

It was the ideal end and also the perfect beginning.

For their life to come.

EPILOGUE

London 1810

"*I* announce the Atharia Women's shelter open," Alessa stated, cutting the bright-purple ribbon with a rapier and watching as it floated to the ground. After three years of building, purchasing furniture, and hiring staff and medical personnel, the shelter was ready to house those who needed help most in London.

Rowan came over to her, kissing her quickly, and she reveled in his presence. She looked back at the building behind them, knowing her wonderful, sweet husband had helped build the center of hope and healing that she prayed the shelter would become.

"Now, you can start preparations on the opening of your next project, my darling, and perhaps take it a little easier. Now that you're expecting, I would like to have you home at a reasonable hour instead of all times of the night."

Alessa chuckled, holding Rowan about the waist and keeping him close. "Perhaps, my dear. We will have to wait and see." Ever since they were married, a month after his arrival in Atharia, she had not spent one night from his side. She had missed him so much. The thought she would spend the rest of her life without him, that to have even a day without seeing his sweet face, was too much.

Her sister had bestowed on them her mother's estate that overlooked the ocean not far from the main palace and within the walls of the royal estate. Their home, as large as it was, was home now. Rowan had settled into life reasonably well, but she sometimes found him doing chores and gardening, tasks that were usually left for the staff to complete.

His grounded soul was a marvel to her, and she loved him that he was so different from her own upbringing. He was not bedazzled by her title or the money he now had access to, the jewels and royal connections. He had married her because he loved her. There was no fear that his only want of her was due to what she could give him.

He would have married her had she been as poor and unfortunate as the women they were set to help in the shelter behind them.

They entered the building where morning tea was set up to celebrate their opening. Alessa had invited several friends of influence, seeking their charity in helping the shelter prosper and grow.

The Duke Sotherton and Aunt Rosemary walked about the bottom half of the shelter, taking in the work and marveling at the facilities that would be available here.

Alessa hoped it would be well-received. She wanted to help those less fortunate than they were. There was nothing better than giving aid. She would much prefer it to receiving gifts.

"I think this is wonderful, Alessa," her younger sister

Princess Elena stated, glancing about the room. "How wonderful of you. I should like to do something similar back home should I decide to stay there."

Rowan took three glasses of champagne, handing one to Alessa and Elena. "Where will you settle if not Atharia?" Rowan asked her.

Elena shrugged her delicate shoulders. "Here in England perhaps, but I have not made up my mind as yet."

Alessa knew her sister was struggling with the decision for her future. She had come out last year, and one year on, she had not shown one iota of interest in any gentleman who had called upon her or sought her out at balls and parties.

She adored reading and kept to herself most of the time, but she was to attend at the end of the London Season a month at Kew Palace, King George's home, even though he was rumored not to be attending the house party himself.

"I see Lady Margaret Villiers is here. I shall go speak with her. I'm to travel down to Kew Place with her next week."

Alessa smiled and watched as her sister joined her friend. She observed her a moment, wondering if Elena ever would find someone as wonderful as she had.

A comforting arm slipped about her waist, squeezing her a little. "She will be fine, Alessa. You are here in England for several more months and will be able to keep a close eye on her. Do not worry," Rowan said, kissing the bridge of her nose.

She grinned, his words already making her feel a lot happier. "I do not know what is wrong with her. In Atharia, before our uncle attempted to take the crown, she was the bubbliest, happiest young woman you would ever meet. She is so withdrawn now. I hope she does not feel alone or that we have abandoned her. Perhaps I have not spent enough time with her since our marriage. I know Holly cannot be expected to since she is the queen, but I am not." Alessa frowned. "I have failed her."

"You have not failed her. That ability is an impossibility for you, no matter who it is in regard to. You help everyone and are always there for anyone, no matter their rank or wealth. Elena will find her way, and if not, I know you will be there for her to guide and assist her when she requires it."

Alessa handed her glass of champagne to a passing footman, preferring to hold her husband instead. She linked her arms about his back, looking up at his fathomless blue eyes that would forever make her forget her own name.

"Have I told you today how much I adore and love you? You really are the perfect husband."

He chuckled, pulling her close. "You were a royal proposition that I could not refuse." He schooled his features, bending down to kiss her, forgetting and not caring who was about them. "I adore you, Alessa. Without you, I do not know who or where I would be. Nowhere good, I can promise you that."

Alessa clasped his jaw, shaking her head. "I do not believe so. You're a strong man and would have found your way in life. I merely stepped in your way and detoured you a bit."

His smile was like a ray of sunshine, and she hoped their children had his features. All of them, so handsome and perfect, as he was to her. "I like detours. Perhaps we ought to detour out of here and to the carriage. The ride home is, I heard, quite long but can be very pleasing with the right company."

She bit her lip, her body thrumming at the thought of being so naughty and leaving early. "I do feel a little tired from all the excitement. Perhaps we ought to make our excuses."

Rowan was already leading her toward the doors. "You're the Princess Alessa of Atharia. What is the point of your privilege if we cannot use it every now and then to our advantage?"

The carriage loomed ahead of them, and one of their liveried footmen opened the door, setting down the steps. "Very true," she agreed, climbing up and settling herself on the squabs.

She heard Rowan give the driver directions, and the carriage lurched forward, taking them home. Rowan pulled her onto his lap, slipping the bodice of her gown down to expose the flesh of her breast.

"Now, where were we, wife?" he asked her, his lips warm, his tongue wicked on her nipple.

She sighed, spiking her fingers into his soft hair. "You're right where you ought to be." Near her heart, where he'd forever be for as long as she lived.

Dear Reader,

Thank you for taking the time to read *A Royal Proposition*! I hope you enjoyed the second book in my new, The Royal House of Atharia series.

I'm so thankful to my readers and your support. If you're able, I would appreciate an honest review of *A Royal Proposition*. As they say, feed an author, leave a review!

If you'd like to learn about book three in my Royal House of Atharia series, *Forever My Princess*, please read on. I have included chapter one for your reading pleasure.

Tamara Gill

FOREVER MY PRINCESS

THE ROYAL HOUSE OF ATHARIA, BOOK 3

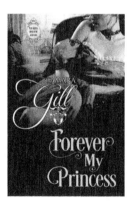

She's not who he thinks she is. But she just might be everything he needs...

Tired doesn't even begin to describe how Princess Elena of Atharia is feeling. A brief respite from the pressures of her position will do her good. Unfortunately, rest isn't something royalty is typically afforded.

But she'll do what is necessary to escape her responsibilities for a time —even if it means becoming someone else entirely…

Lord Theodore Ward has no love for the wealthy. But if he doesn't marry well soon, he'll lose everything. And his hunt for a perfect bride cannot begin while his mother is unwell and unattended. So, hiring a lady's companion is the only option. Then the lovely Elena Smith arrives at his door and his plans become infinitely more complicated…

When all the truths and secrets come to light, can these opposites find their way to happily ever after? Or will Theo lose his princess forever?

CHAPTER 1

*P*rincess Elena of Atharia sat in the opulent wingback chair in her sister's new London home and waited for her friend Lady Margaret Villiers to arrive.

She had sent word almost two hours ago for her to call, and yet still, she had not arrived. Elena stood, pacing back and forth between her chair and the mantle, the clock clicking down the time with an annoying click.

What could have kept her? Margaret had not sent word that she could not attend her summons.

Elena frowned. For her plan to work, she needed Margaret's loyalty and silence for the next month at least. The crinkle of the many letters she had written crackled in her pocket, and she patted her leg, ensuring herself they were still there.

She had spent hours penning them, wanting to ensure her sister Alessa never assumed she was not where she was supposed to be. That she would not come looking for her for the next month at least.

A footman knocked and came into the room, bowing.

"Your highness, Lady Margaret Villiers wishes an audience."

Elena whirled about, seeing her friend grinning behind the footman's back. "Thank you, John. We will have tea if you please," she commanded the footman, watching as Margaret came into the room and closed the door behind her.

Elena met her across the room, taking her friend's hands. "Oh, I'm so very pleased you are here. I did not think you would attend, and then I was not sure what I would do."

Margaret, sensing the worry in Elena's tone, frowned. "Whatever is the matter that you are all aflutter? I thought you would be busy packing for Kew Palace? What fun we shall have for the next month. Do you think King George will attend after all?"

Elena gestured toward a chair. "We need to talk, please sit, Margaret," she asked her friend, joining her on the settee.

"What is it that you need to discuss so urgently?" Margaret slumped. "Are you about to tell me you're not going to attend the house party? I shall be ever so disappointed if you do not."

Guilt pricked her conscience that her friend's concern was about to come to fruition. But there was no way around it. She needed to leave London to remove herself from the endless cycle of balls and parties. Having entered society last year in Atharia, Elena felt she had done nothing but parade herself before young men who were looking for a bride.

She no longer wanted to play such games. A month away at a country house with an elderly lady was just what she needed to regain her composure, to prepare herself for a union that would eventually come.

She was not fooled enough not to know that she would eventually marry a man that her sisters deemed appropriate. But it was not how she wanted to choose a spouse. She wanted to fall in love, to marry her best friend. The gentlemen in town were all so charming and complimentary, so much so that their constant flattery made her teeth ache they were so sweet.

And false, she admitted.

"I'm afraid I'm going to disappoint you, Margaret dear, but I do hope you'll support me as your dearest friend, for I shall need your help, even if I'm not with you at Kew Palace."

"What do you need me to do? Or better yet," Margaret added, "what is it that you're going to do?"

"As to that," Elena said, nerves and expectation making her stomach flip. She had never been adventurous. After being left at the castle in Atharia when her sister Alessa had escaped, she had done all she could to become invisible.

Such a temperament and desire had not left her since coming out and being in society. She was no longer so comfortable in boisterous and crowded ballrooms. She would much prefer a country ride or a long walk in beautiful gardens to a ball.

"I have taken a position as a ladies companion to Dowager Marchioness Lyon in Somerset. I will be working for her ladyship under the alias as Miss Elena Smith. I leave for the estate tomorrow, the same day I'm supposed to leave for the house party."

Margaret's mouth gaped, and Elena hoped she had not

bitten off too much for her friend to take in or for her to do. "Tell me you're willing to help me. I truly do not wish to attend the house party. I need some time away from London and the madness that my title brings into my life. A month in the county will be the perfect escape, and I shall return in four weeks, ready to find a husband and marry."

"Really?" Margaret stated, raising one disbelieving brow. "But what of Lord Lyon? Will he not be home? From what I know of him, he never attends the Season, something about a rift that happened years ago with his father here in London."

"That does not mean he does not need a companion for his mother, but from what the correspondence has stated so far, forwarded to me from the servant registry office I've been hired through, he is to return to town."

"Well," Margaret said with a surprised sigh. "I did not think he would ever come to London. He is one of those country gentlemen who never comes to town, but I'm sure his return here will cause a lot of hearts to flutter."

Elena did not care how many hearts fluttered in London for the marquess, so long as she had a lovely, relaxing four weeks looking after his mother and keeping her company. A month of long country walks, of reading and sitting before the fire, not having to attend a ball or soiree, or a royal event would be a pleasure indeed.

"Perhaps he intends to find a wife, like so many other gentlemen of our acquaintance. Nevertheless, his plans are not my concern. I have been hired as Miss Smith and Miss Smith I shall be for the next four weeks."

Margaret pinned her with a disapproving stare. "And may I ask how it is, Princess Elena," she said, accentuating her title, "that you will get away with such a plan? Your sister is in London and will want to know that you are safe and well, especially after her own safety scare last Season. I do not see how you can get away with this foolery at all."

Elena had it all planned and was the reason why she had asked Margaret to call today, for she too featured in her escape. She reached into her pocket and pulled out the six letters she had written to Alessa. "You know that I adore you as a friend, but I do need your help if I'm to succeed. Will you help me?"

Margaret's mouth opened and closed several times, her eyes wide with surprise. "Me?" she said, pointing to herself. "What is it that I'm supposed to do. Need I remind you that you have a sister who is a Queen and another who is a very independent, strong-willed princess right here in town. Should either of them find out I helped you escape, I shall be strung up and hung from the nearest gallows."

Elena chuckled. "I can always count on you to make me laugh, but you are wrong. Neither sister will ever find out. If you can have these letters sent over the next four weeks while you're at Kew Palace, Alessa will be none the wiser. She will not know that I'm in Somerset at all."

"And if your sister calls in at Kew Palace. The estate is not so very far away from London."

Elena waved her friend's concerns away. "She is far too busy with her charities to be worried about me at a house party for a month. While I have little doubt that she will lecture me to behave and remember my manners before I go, she will never think that I shall not attend at all."

And what of King George who sent out all these invitations. Will he not out you to your siblings?"

"No," Elena stated, shaking her head and not the least concerned with that part of her plan either. "King George will not attend, even if he has invited us all to his country estate. You know he prefers to keep his select few and himself locked away at Windsor."

"Even so, I feel nervous about deceiving your sisters. They will be ever so cross with me should they find out."

Elena reached out and took Margaret's hand. "Listen, they will not be angry with you; they will be angry with me." She reached back into her pocket and pulled out another letter. "This is all the information of where I am and the dates. Lord Lyon was very particular as to the time that he required a companion for his mama, and it was perfect luck that they coincided with the house party at Kew. Do not worry at all. You enjoy your time away from town, hand these letters to a footman at the palace, and that is all you need to concern yourself with."

When Margaret entered on indecision, Elena wondered if she had been foolish in thinking she could do such a thing. To run away, even if only for four weeks, was still a risk. Her heart went out to her friend, worrying so. "If you do not wish to, that is perfectly well too, Margaret. I would never ask you to do anything that you're uncomfortable or disagree with. I can change my plans and come to the house party, and no one would ever be the wiser to what I wanted to do."

Margaret bit her bottom lip in thought. "No, I shall help you. You are my closest friend, and you deserve to do what you think will make you ready for marriage. An institution that we all shall have to face very soon I should imagine. I want to help you, and I shall post your letters. But," Margaret said, stemming Elena from pulling her into a hug. "Should your sisters arrive and enquire of your whereabouts or want to see you, I will tell them the truth. Are you in agreement?" she asked her, holding up her hand and sticking out her smallest finger.

"What are you doing with your hand?" Elena asked, having never seen anyone hold out their finger in such a way.

"This is a piggy promise. Should you shake my finger with your own smallest finger, it will mean that you agree to my terms, and you are free to travel to Somerset and Lord Lyon's estate."

Elena stared at her friend's smallest digit, thinking over her friend's terms, which were utterly appropriate and fair. She hooked her finger around Margarets. "I swear and agree to what you say, and I thank you so very much."

Hope and excitement thrummed through her veins over her forthcoming month away from town, from people and noise, scandal and negotiation. How wonderful her time in Somerset would be, and tomorrow morning when the carriage arrived to take her away, she would be ready and willing to transform into Miss Elena Smith, Princess Elena no more.

Want to read more? Purchase, Forever My Princess today!

SERIES BY TAMARA GILL

The Wayward Woodvilles

Royal House of Atharia

League of Unweddable Gentlemen

Kiss the Wallflower

Lords of London

To Marry a Rogue

A Time Traveler's Highland Love

A Stolen Season

Scandalous London

High Seas & High Stakes

Daughters Of The Gods

Stand Alone Books

DEFIANT SURRENDER

TO SIN WITH SCANDAL

OUTLAWS

ABOUT THE AUTHOR

Tamara is an Australian author who grew up in an old mining town in country South Australia, where her love of history was founded. So much so, she made her darling husband travel to the UK for their honeymoon, where she dragged him from one historical monument and castle to another.

A mother of three, her two little gentlemen in the making, a future lady (she hopes) and a part-time job keep her busy in the real world, but whenever she gets a moment's peace she loves to write romance novels in an array of genres, including regency, medieval and time travel.

www.tamaragill.com
tamaragillauthor@gmail.com

Printed in Great Britain
by Amazon